BREED

One of the largest sl...
resisting all attempts ... finally it
reached the exposed ear. The monstrous creature
fixed its mouth parts firmly inside Prince's ear and
began feeding, boring deeper. Towards the brain.

The dog at last tried to run but the sheer weight of
his attackers slowed his flight and he could only crawl
as more and more slugs found their way onto his body
and set to work with their teeth, sucking his warm
blood which filled their bodies, pumping them up
like leeches until it seemed they would burst.

From the pipe in the floor yet more slugs emerged.
A never-ending black torrent of death . . .

Also by Shaun Hutson and available in Sphere Books:

SHAUN HUTSON

Breeding Ground

SPHERE BOOKS LTD

To Bob Tanner the man who first lifted the
stone and invited me to crawl out from under it.
Thank you.

A SPHERE Book

First published in Great Britain in 1985 by
Star Books, a Division of W. H. Allen & Co plc
This edition published in 1990 by Sphere Books Ltd
1st reprint 1990

ISBN 0 7474 0780 0

Reproduced, printed and bound in Great Britain by
BPCC Hazell Books
Aylesbury, Bucks, England
Member of BPCC Ltd.

Sphere Books Ltd
A Division of
Macdonald & Co (Publishers) Ltd
Orbit House
1 New Fetter Lane
London EC4A 1AR
A member of Maxwell Macmillan Pergamon Publishing Corporation

'Close the city and tell the people
that something is coming to call' . . .'
– *Ronnie James Dio*

Acknowledgements

I would like to thank Mr Greg Teckover of the Metropolitan Water Authority for his help. Also, thankyou to Mr Paul Hayers. Special thanks, as ever, to everyone at W.H. Allen. Also, for different reasons, thankyou to Niki (the only lady I know who managed to turn watering house plants into a health hazard). To Chris and Kim at Ripple Records; to Dave Risby (it's a fair cop); to Belinda (who really ought to be careful where she stubs her cigarettes out) but, most of all thanks to YOU, the reader. To everyone who's ever parted with some of their cash to buy one of my books, I thank you.

Shaun Hutson

Prologue

The farmer watched impatiently as the crates of lettuce were unloaded from the back of his lorry. He chewed the end of his pipe, which, as ever, remained unlit.

All around him the place was alive with the sounds of crashing boxes, raised voices and laughter. The usual cacophony which accompanied the early-morning proceedings at Covent Garden.

The summer sun was already high in the sky above London, pouring its unrelenting heat down over the capital. The day promised to be another scorcher.

The farmer disliked the city. He'd lived in the country all his life and the frenzied hustle and bustle which characterized the sprawling metropolis unsettled him. He shifted the unlit pipe to the other side of his mouth, watching as his produce was inspected. The buyer moved from crate to crate, swiftly but expertly checking the contents. Occasionally he would remove one of the lettuces, tossing it onto a nearby pile of other discarded vegetables.

'Good crop again,' said the farmer.

'Yeah, only a few bad ones,' murmured the buyer, picking up another lettuce.

Noticing something inside the inner leaves, he threw it onto the pile with the other rejects.

After fifteen minutes he was finished. The deal was concluded and the farmer climbed thankfully back into the lorry. He waved farewell to the buyer and set off to battle his way through the traffic, anxious to get home to the relative peace of his farm.

As the day progressed, the pile of discarded vegetables grew higher until it was almost as tall as a man. The heat of the sun caused the green stuff to wilt and a powerful smell began to rise from it, but those nearby ignored the stench.

Stallholders shouted out their prices and bickered with their rivals. It was a normal day.

No one noticed the lettuce which lay near the bottom of the pile, rejected because of the strange cylindrical objects inside its inner leaves. The transparent mucoid tubes with the black centres.

Despite the searing heat of the sun the tiny shapes glistened as if perpetually wet and, slowly, as if triggered by some secret, silent alarm, they began to split open. One by one the liquescent tubes disgorged their contents.

The slugs were less than one centimetre long, almost transparent and already covered by a thin film of slime. Against the dark, rotting vegetation they were barely visible and they remained in one gently moving cluster no bigger than a matchbox.

They grew swiftly. Much more swiftly than normal, and with that growth came another change.

At first almost invisible, they began to darken in colour. A pale, pus coloured yellow first, then a light brown. They remained clotted together, hidden within the wrinkled folds of the lettuce.

And they grew.

Though still smaller than a finger nail, by noon they had doubled in size.

Tuesday – the 11th

One

The half-eaten hamburger was still warm and Tommy Price smiled to himself as he stuffed it into his mouth, oblivious to the revolted stares of a passing woman who had seen him plunge his hand into the waste-bin and retrieve the food. He chewed quickly, wiped his hands on his jacket and then peered into the bin once more, rummaging around in the rubbish in search of something else to satisfy his raging hunger. He found nothing, however. Muttering to himself, he moved on to the next bin and dug his hand in like a child at a lucky dip. The search yielded a half-full carton of milkshake, but when Tommy removed the plastic lid he saw that the thick liquid was covered by a rancid sheath of grey-green mould. Flies buzzed around him, one settling on the rim of the carton, savouring the sweet curdled fluid. Tommy dropped the milkshake back into the bin.

In the cloudless blue sky, the sun hung like a ball of fire, baking all below it with fierce rays. As Tommy walked, the pavement felt hot beneath his feet, the warmth having little difficulty reaching his bare soles through shoes which were nearly worn through. As he made his way along the Strand he paused at each waste-bin and performed his familiar ritual, hunting through the rubbish for anything vaguely edible. During the last four or five weeks he had discovered that the human digestive system was capable of absorbing almost anything. Especially if its owner was nearly starving.

Even though he had not eaten a good meal for nearly two months, Tommy did not seem to have lost much weight. He was a powerfully-built individual, standing around six feet,

11

the jacket he wore stretched almost to breaking point across his broad back and shoulders. The cuffs were frayed, the elbows shiny and it bore numerous stains. His trousers, once part of a suit, were too short and the unfashionably wide bottoms could not conceal his filthy socks which puckered round his ankles like surgical stockings.

Tommy Price walked on up the road, sometimes bumping into tourists and shoppers, although they did their best to avoid him. Tommy didn't smell very good, especially in such hot weather. He ran a hand through his hair which hadn't been washed for weeks, wincing as his fingers touched a large spot just below his hairline. He caught sight of his reflection in a shop window and paused for a moment, taken aback by the sight which greeted him. It was like looking at another person, someone alien to him. He wondered if the apparition would vanish if he blinked. He tried and it didn't. The same unkempt reflection continued to stare back at him.

He had been in London for the last two months since leaving Newcastle, and it had been eight weeks of misery. The pit where he had worked since he was sixteen had closed down over a year ago, and at the age of forty-seven he had found himself on the scrap heap, like so many of his generation. He remembered the stories his father had told him of the great march from Jarrow in 1926. Now he, like his father, had come to London but for different reasons.

Tommy did not, like many misinformed youngsters, believe that he would find a fortune in the country's capital, but he had at least expected some work. He didn't care what it was. Nothing had come his way, however. His savings had dwindled and, within two weeks of arriving, he had found himself seeking shelter in Salvation Army Hostels. And now he could not even find solace there any longer.

Tommy liked his drink. If he had to steal it then that was fair enough, but he needed it. He'd been caught trying to liberate a bottle of Haig from an off-licence, and owing to his circumstances the judge had dismissed the case. But Tommy had been desperate, and the sight of two five-pound notes in the pocket of another man at the hostel that night had been too much of a temptation. He'd been banned after being caught. Now he walked the streets every day, carrying his belongings in a battered hold-all and searching dustbins and hotel rubbish skips and pub yards for what meagre pickings there were.

He had thought once or twice of returning to Newcastle but there was nothing there for him any more. He was without a family. He had never married. Both his parents were dead, his younger brother had been killed in a pit accident at twenty-four, and his sister now lived in Canada with her husband and children. He pushed the thoughts of the past out of his mind, surprised at how easily they disappeared. It was as if he had been traipsing these London streets all his life, foraging like some kind of carrion crow, accepting anything and everything edible. He had suffered from a stomach upset at the beginning, but now his belly seemed immune to whatever vile garbage he chose to inflict upon it.

Tommy wiped the sweat from his face with one grime-encrusted hand and walked on. Another five minutes and he had reached his destination.

Covent Garden seemed unusually busy on this blistering summer's day but Tommy moved purposefully through the crowds, peering longingly at the fruit and vegetables laid out on stalls all around him. He paused to inspect a waste-bin and his face lit up as he found a bottle of Guinness. The neck was broken and jagged, but Tommy raised it to his lips and drank. The dark fluid was warm and sour but he swallowed most of it, wiping his mouth with the back of his hand before moving on. He belched loudly and his stomach rumbled protestingly. Tommy took another swig from the bottle, aware now of a particularly rank odour which assaulted his nostrils.

Just ahead of him he saw a pile of fruit and vegetables, discarded by the stallholders in the market. Without hesitation he crossed to it and began grabbing handfuls of the sub-standard produce. His fingers sank into a rotted tomato but he merely wiped the orange mush on his jacket and pushed some more food into his hold-all.

'What are you doing, mate?' a voice asked and Tommy

13

turned to see a broad man, stripped to the waist, standing before him.

'You don't want this, do you?' Tommy said, indicating the pile of discarded food.

'Help yourself,' the man told him and wandered away.

Tommy continued his little harvest, ignoring the hordes of flies which swarmed round the reeking mound. He picked up a handful of small potatoes and pushed them into his pocket.

The lettuce he dropped into his hold-all.

The leaves were wilting but it was moist, perhaps a little sticky, he thought. Tommy saw something glistening on the leaves, shining brightly in the sunshine, but he paid it no heed.

Inside the lettuce, the small slugs remained in their tight bundle, held firmly together by the thick coating of slime which surrounded them like some kind of gelatinous cocoon.

Finally, his pockets and hold-all stuffed with the discarded fruit and vegetables, Tommy left the remaining garbage to the flies and wasps which swarmed over it like an undulating cloud.

He left the traders and their customers behind, seeking out the nearest empty doorway in which to enjoy his feast. There was a shop close by, its windows boarded up. Paint had been sprayed all over the wood and Tommy glanced briefly at the grafitti:

IF THATCHER WAS THE ANSWER IT MUST HAVE BEEN A FUCKING STUPID QUESTION

99% IS SHIT

Why give the other 1% the benefit of the doubt? thought Tommy, seating himself in the darkened doorway amongst the yellowed newspaper and discarded cigarette packets. He rummaged through one and found a more or less intact Marlboro. This was his lucky day. Except for the fact that he had nothing to light it with. He put it in his breast pocket for future use and settled down with the food he'd scavenged just minutes before. He still had some Guinness left in the broken bottle, too.

He devoured the food ravenously, ignoring the sometimes

rancid flavours. It filled his stomach and that was all that mattered.

He pushed lumps of the lettuce into his mouth, swallowing large pieces of it whole.

A vile taste suddenly filled his mouth, and for a moment he thought he was going to vomit. His stomach contracted as something thick and slimy touched the back of his throat before sliding down. He licked his tongue around his mouth and lips, spitting out some viscous fluid which looked like mucus. He coughed and spat again, reaching for the bottle of Guinness, which he downed in one long swallow in an effort to wash away the foul taste. He threw away what remained of the lettuce, rubbing his stomach. After a moment or two the taste seemed to fade away and he got to his feet, belching loudly once again. It was more than he'd eaten for a week. Tommy fumbled in his pocket and found the cigarette, then wandered off in search of a light.

The sun had reached its zenith. The city sweltered beneath the merciless onslaught of heat.

Tommy took off his jacket as he walked, enjoying the feel of the sun on his skin.

It was another two hours before the pains began.

Almost reluctantly, as if loath to give up its domination of the heavens, the sun sank lower in the sky and darker skies signalled the onset of evening. The clouds above London were stained purple and crimson and layered one on top of another. The rich colours spread across the sky like ink soaking into blotting paper. Tall buildings became featureless black monoliths against the multi-hued backdrop.

In London's West End, however, the streets were bright. The glow of thousands of light bulbs and strands of neon created an artificial, many-coloured day which lit all but the darkest corners and alleyways. And the ceaseless activity, if anything, seemed to intensify as people went about their pleasure and, in some cases, business. The night people were out.

Some were buying, some were selling.

Tommy Price moved slowly down Regent Street, his face pale and expressionless, one hand clutched tightly to his stomach.

The pain had begun, he estimated, soon after three o'clock that afternoon. Slight nagging discomfort at first, centred around his navel, a griping annoyance which he had expected to leave him. But now, six hours later, the pain had grown to almost unbearable intensity, gnawing away at him relentlessly until it felt as if his entire torso, even his bowels, were filled with fire. He walked unsteadily, with a drunkard's gait, and more than once he attracted stares from passing policemen. But no one stopped him as he careered on down the street, past shops now closed, past the Rent boys who waited at the exit of Piccadilly Tube station. The buyers and sellers.

Tommy blundered across the road, narrowly avoiding a collision with a motor-cyclist, stumbling up the kerb on the other side, almost losing his footing. He stood still for long moments, aware only of the agonizing pain which gripped him like a steel fist, the fingers tightening by the second. He felt a wave of violent nausea wrack his body and it was all he could do to prevent himself from vomiting. He leant against the window of a nearby Wimpey Bar, gazing in at a group of young children, one of whom stuck his tongue out at the ghastly apparition looking through the glass at him. The other children laughed and pointed at Tommy, who whirled away, banging into a tall youth in a camouflage jacket.

The youth grunted and pushed Tommy, who staggered and fell.

Passers-by kept well away from him, although one or two stopped to look at him as he crouched helplessly on the pavement, clutching his stomach.

He groaned as a wave of pain so intense it almost caused him to scream aloud shook him and, this time, he could not contain himself. His stomach contracted and a foul-smelling stream of vomit gushed from his mouth and splattered on the pavement. Those standing nearby hurried on. Two young girls laughed disgustedly but Tommy did not hear what they

16

said because just then a second spasm shook him and another stream of hideously-coloured liquid flooded from him, puddling in thick clots on the pavement. He tried to rise, reeking streamers of thick vomit and mucus hanging from his lips and chin. Through eyes blurred with pain he saw that there were dark streaks in the puddle of vomit before him. And, along with the bitter taste, he also detected that of blood. He wiped his mouth, his breath catching in his throat as he saw the crimson liquid glistening on the back of his hand. The sight of it made him want to be sick again but he managed to control himself, rising with a monumental effort of will. He tried to straighten up but the pain dug white-hot knives into his belly, groin and chest. He struggled a few more yards then slumped against a wall, his breath coming in agonized gasps. A voice close by told him to move on and he saw that he was propped against the glass window of a cinema cash-desk. The cashier, a short thin woman with thick spectacles, shouted at him once more to move away and, as a burly-looking doorman approached, Tommy managed to do so.

As he crossed the road figures swam before him as if he were looking through a heat haze. He saw the expressions on their faces as they looked at him, his jacket and trousers stained with vomit and blood. He saw the disgust, the bewilderment. Even the amusement. He felt like crying out to one of these people for help but he knew it would be futile for, indeed, how *could* they help him? Could they stop the pain he was feeling? The screaming agony which made him feel as if his intestines were being knotted repeatedly by red hot fingers. Clutching his stomach with both hands, he lurched on towards Leicester Square, the lights from the Swiss Centre winking invitingly at him as he drew nearer. There were wooden benches outside the building. Perhaps if he could reach one of those and sit down...

Tommy practically ran towards the benches, almost falling onto the nearest one. He doubled up in pain again, tears of suffering running down his grimy cheeks. Behind him a small crowd had gathered around a man who was playing a saxophone in the street. Mellow, soothing notes floated up on the warm evening air, but they did nothing to sooth the pain which Tommy felt. He sat a moment longer, then wrenched himself upright once more, passing a middle-aged couple who stood and watched as he stumbled away.

He made his way across Leicester Square, the lights which shone from the front of the Empire Cinema dazzling him. There were many youngsters there, seated on the walls which surrounded a variety of small trees and shrubs dotted around the concrete expanse. Some of the kids followed his stumbling progress indifferently as he headed for the entrance to the public lavatory.

At the top of the steps Tommy steadied himself, slowing his pace in case he should slip and fall. Step by step he descended, the pain now beyond belief. He felt as if his entire torso was contracting, then expanding, swelling as if ready to burst. He felt the nausea building once more, a tidal wave of pain which he knew was unstoppable. Tommy rolled the last few feet down the steps and sprawled on the wet floor, blood dribbling in a thin ribbon from one corner of his mouth.

A man standing at the urinal looked round in surprise and alarm. So anxious was he to be away from this frightful-looking apparition, he almost wet himself pushing his penis back into his trousers. He whipped up his zip, wincing as he caught a pubic hair in his haste, and sprinted up the stairs, leaving Tommy sprawled on the tiles.

Tommy began to crawl towards one of the cubicles, inch by agonizing inch, his lower body and chest ablaze with pain, blood spilling onto the dirty tiles, spreading out like blossoming crimson flowers. He felt his stomach lurch again but he clenched his teeth, his mouth filling with vomit which forced his cheeks to bulge until, at last, he let it go in a fetid spray of blood flecked yellow ooze which spattered the cubicle and the toilet itself. Head bowed over the bowl, he emptied his stomach until blood began to colour the water. Thick crimson fluid coated the cracked porcelain and spilled down Tommy's chin and chest. He tried to scream but the blood and vomit clogged in his throat. He felt something warm and wet running from his anus but he didn't realize that this was blood as well.

He couldn't breathe. His head felt as if it were being pumped full of air and, all the time, the pain in his stomach intensified until he prayed for death to come and release him from the insufferable torment.

That death seemed to be a long time coming.

The cubicle door swung shut behind him.

Two

'Look, I'm telling you, they lock this place up at twelve,' Paul Hilston said, looking around the deserted lavatory.

'Then we've got another hour, haven't we?' Howard Mallows chided him. 'Have you got the fucking stuff or what?'

Hilston nodded, clutching a large brown paper bag to his chest.

'The fucking police come down here at night you know,' he said, agitatedly. 'I ain't getting caught with this lot.' He held up the bag.

'Well, if you're scared, piss off now. Right?'

'I ain't scared.'

'Then get the fucking stuff out, before some nob-head walks in,' demanded Mallows. 'Let's go in one of the cubicles.'

They both stepped into the furthest one and slid the bolt. Mallows lowered the seat and planted himself on it, watching as Hilston opened the brown bag and took out two tubes of Bostik and two smaller, plastic bags. He handed a tube of glue and one of the bags to his companion, who unscrewed the top of the tube and began squeezing the thick fluid into the plastic bag.

Mallows was smiling broadly, revealing a set of teeth which hadn't encountered toothpaste for some time. He was twenty, his face pock-marked and deeply pitted. There were dark scabs around both his nostrils and he picked at one as he squeezed the glue into the bag. His hair cut short, accentuating the size of his ears, which stuck out prominently from a head which looked too small for his body. The jeans he wore were cut short to show off his long boots. The red laces matched his T-shirt.

Hilston was a year or so younger. A thin, foxy looking lad with smooth, almost feminine skin which had yet to feel a razor's edge. His hair, however, was even shorter than Mallows' and a little lighter, making him appear almost bald. He waited while his companion emptied the last of the Bostik into the bag, tossed the tube away and then scrunched up the plastic to form a nozzle. This he placed over his nose and mouth. He inhaled, then exhaled deeply, never allowing the bag to leave his face. Hilston watched for a moment longer then followed his example.

It was the first time he'd ever sniffed and the initial dose of fumes made him cough, but he tried again despite the fact that his eyes had begun to water. It felt as if someone had stuck a lighted match up each of his nostrils. The smell seemed to fill his head, and for a second he swayed and thought he was going to faint, but as he kept breathing he found that a pleasantly light-headed feeling was beginning to engulf him.

For his part, Mallows sat back on the toilet seat, his face still buried in the bag. When he lowered it, his nose and the skin around his mouth were bright red. He chuckled and looked at his companion.

'Fucking great, eh?' he said, his voice distant and slightly slurred.

Hilston nodded and dropped his own bag.

'It's better when you get out in the air,' Mallows added. 'Come on.' He got to his feet and slid back the bolt on the door, and they both walked out into the dimly-lit lavatory, which as far as they could see was still deserted. The glue tubes lay discarded in the cubicle.

'What if the filth are around?' asked Hilston. 'They'll smell it on us.'

'Fuck them,' said Mallows, kicking the door of the cubicle next to him. He went to each one in turn and repeated the mindless action, chuckling to himself. When he reached the last one the door swung back only a foot or so. He kicked it again, feeling resistance on the other side.

Both of them stood still for a moment as if taken aback by the temporary obstruction. Then Mallows kicked the door again, the impact of boot on wood echoing loudly in the silent cavern.

'There's somebody in there,' Hilston announced, dropping to one knee. He could see a dark form inside, hunched close to the lavatory bowl. In the gloom it was difficult to distinguish colours and the glue was further affecting his vision, but he could make out a pool of dark liquid around the base of the bowl, some of which had trickled beneath the door.

'Perhaps he's got diarrhoea,' Mallows chuckled. Then, kicking the door again, he shouted, 'Come on mate, it's time to go home.'

The thick wooden partition moved another couple of inches, enabling Mallows to squeeze his considerable bulk into the cubicle. He looked down at the man slumped before him. Now he could see the filthy, vomit-spattered jacket and trousers, the matted hair and the unearthly paleness of the skin made all the worse by the dull glare of the fluorescents in the lavatory.

'Leave him,' Hilston said. 'Let's go. Come on.'

'Had a few too many have you, mate?' Mallows chuckled, looking down at the ragged mess before him.

Tommy Price did not move.

'Howard, come on,' said Hilston again, peering over his friend's shoulder. 'He's pissed out of his fucking mind, you can see that.'

Mallows shot his companion an angry glance.

'He might have got some money, you prat,' snapped the

21

older youth. Then he returned his attention to Tommy once more, nudging him with the toe of his boot.

'Oi, wake up,' he said, prodding him again.

There was no response.

'Leave it out, Howard,' Hilston insisted. 'He's right out of it.' Then, for some reason, he began laughing. 'He don't look like he's got any fucking money, does he?'

Mallows seemed unconcerned about the dark liquid which surrounded Tommy, congealing on the dirty floor like drying paint. The big youth kicked at the motionless man's legs, the force of his blows increasing with each kick.

'Wake up, you cunt,' he hissed, transferring his attention to Tommy's upper body. He pushed him with the sole of his boot, watching as the body merely slid down onto the floor, the pale face tilted upwards, eyes closed. Mallows rubbed his eyes, his head swimming. He sniffed back some mucus and gritted his teeth, made a hawking noise and spat a thick green globule at Tommy. It hit his cheek and rolled down like a huge sticky tear.

Enraged by his failure to arouse any movement in the tramp, Mallows stepped back, preparing to strike harder.

'I'll wake you up, you bastard,' he snarled and drove his foot forward with as much force as he could muster.

The boot struck Tommy in the stomach.

The flesh and muscles seemed merely to burst and, as his shirt split open, so too did his lower torso. From pelvis to sternum, the body seemed to rupture, like some kind of pea pod. The entire cavity opened like a pair of obscene lips, sliding back to welcome the intruding boot of Mallows which disappeared into the seething mess inside. Flesh tore like fabric and the skinhead almost overbalanced as his foot sank into the tramp's body, forcing its way through to the spine, such was the force of the impact.

His eyes widened in horror as he looked down.

Hilston tried to scream but he could only stand riveted, wondering, for precious seconds, if he was hallucinating.

He wished that he had been.

Slugs filled the riven torso like maggots in an open wound,

slithering over one another, their thick slime mingling with blood and the spilled green bile which had oozed from Tommy's gall bladder. The hideous black creatures, some as long as six inches, looked as if they had been sealed together by the glutinous muck which covered them. Like a huge black carnivorous cancer which had grown inside the tramp, literally devouring his internal organs, eating him away from the inside. Until now, at last, aided by Mallows' boot, they had burst forth.

Tommy's lips moved soundlessly and Mallows watched, mesmerized, as a thick black shape nudged its way free of his mouth. The slug's eye stalks extended slowly, and as it slithered down the pale face of its host, another followed it, then another.

A smaller rent opened at the hollow of Tommy's throat and still another slug emerged, blood also running from the cut as it ate its way free. The writhing forms inside the torso seemed to move as one, spilling from the gaping hole with a sickening slurping sound which seemed all the louder because of the silence. Blood and fragments of uneaten intestine flowed forward with them, carried on the reeking carpet of black bodies which began to move towards the watching skinheads.

Mallows felt his bowels loosen, felt something soft and warm splatter his underpants. The stench of his own excrement mingled with the vile smell which rose from the slugs like a noxious cloud. Those that had emerged from the throat and mouth of Tommy Price were now busy devouring the wasted face, burrowing through the eyes and upwards into the brain. Others fastened themselves to the bloated lips and began feeding on the soft flesh and clotted fluid within.

Mallows turned and ran, knocking Hilston over in his efforts to escape this nightmare vision. Hilston got up and turned to follow, doubling up as he did, his stomach finally surrendering to the contractions which tore through him. He unleashed a stream of vomit as he ran, almost slipping over in it. His footsteps clattered frantically up the steps.

Finally the lavatory was in silence again, except for the obscene sucking sounds made by the horde of slugs as they continued to slither from the body of the tramp until only a huge cavity remained, the bones of the ribcage shining white through the blood and slime where internal organs had once been. Like the sloughed skin of a snake the body was now merely an empty shell, and the face had been decimated by those slugs as yet unsatiated. Both eye sockets were empty now and the mouth yawned open like a black chasm to reveal that even the tongue had been eaten.

The leading slugs, the larger ones, hauled their bloated forms across the soiled floor of the lavatory, followed by their smaller companions. An undulating slimy mass which left a glistening trail of mucus behind, they moved easily and surprisingly quickly across the floor and slipped into the trough at the base of the urinals. They crawled or floated in the yellow stream of urine, allowing themselves to be sucked down into the pipes which eventually deposited them in the sewers far below. The darkness seemed to welcome them, and in the blackness they were invisible.

Above, the last few slithered down the pipe and out of sight. There were perhaps a hundred of them.

There would soon be many more.

Three

The smell was almost overpowering. A fetid combination of urine, excrement and vomit but also something more powerful. More pungent. The smell of death.

It was a smell which Detective Inspector Ray Grogan knew only too well, and he recognized it as soon as he entered the lavatory in Leicester Square.

A flashbulb exploded, momentarily illuminating the

24

subterranean cavern with cold white light. Grogan winced slightly and slowed his pace as he reached the bottom of the stairs. He dug into his pocket, produced a breath freshener and aimed it at his mouth. The peppermint spray missed and went up his nose. Muttering to himself, Grogan tried again and succeeded, then dropped the spray back into his pocket. He looked around him at the two uniformed men and three plain-clothes policemen who were also present. A photographer was standing just ahead of him taking pictures of the tiled floor outside one cubicle. At the far end of the row, another plain-clothes man was collecting exhibits. The man was wearing a corduroy jacket worn at the elbows. His hair was long, almost reaching the collar of his blue shirt. He wore brown slacks which needed turning up an inch or two. When the man saw Grogan he turned and walked towards him.

The two men exchanged greetings and Grogan's colleague lit a cigarette. Detective Sergeant Martin Nicholson offered one to his superior.

'I've given up,' Grogan reminded him, trying to ignore the smell of smoke as it wafted towards him. He sighed. 'Well, what have we got? It'd better be worth dragging me out of bed at this hour.'

Grogan checked his watch again and saw that it was just after 1.00 a.m. Then he followed Nicholson to one of the cubicles and peered in.

'Oh Christ,' he murmured.

The photographer stepped aside to allow the DI a better look at the remains of Tommy Price.

Grogan ran a quick appraising eye over the corpse, or what remained of it, his stomach churning slightly as he gazed first at the empty eye sockets, then at the gaping hole in the torso. He turned to look at Nicholson.

'Who is he?' the DI wanted to know.

'We don't know. He wasn't carrying any ID. Or if he was it was taken.'

'It doesn't exactly look like a mugging, does it?' Grogan said, cryptically. 'What about fingerprints? Dental records?'

'They'll be checked as soon as Forensics get started.'

Grogan nodded, massaging the back of his neck with one broad, powerful-looking hand.

'Who found him?' he wanted to know.

'One of our uniformed blokes,' Nicholson said. 'He was checking down here around midnight...' He allowed the sentence to trail off. 'I've never seen anything like it before.'

'Join the club.' Grogan peered around the door of the cubicle once more, his eyes drawn to the gutted corpse. 'What's that stuff on his face?'

'It looks like mucus of some kind. It's everywhere. Look.' He motioned to the tiles beneath their feet and the sticky fluid which glittered with a vile lustre beneath the blinking fluorescent. 'We found this as well, in one of the other cubicles.' Nicholson held up the bag he'd been holding to reveal the empty tubes of Bostik. 'We should be able to get some prints off these. It might give us some kind of clue.'

Grogan nodded slowly, stroking his chin contemplatively.

'It could have been a couple of kids,' Nicholson offered. 'If they'd been sniffing, you never know. I'd just like to know what sort of weapon they used.'

Grogan entered the cubicle and crouched down beside the body of Tommy Price, his gaze travelling to the dead man's hands.

'There aren't any defence cuts on the hands,' said the DI. He looked at the dried vomit which had crusted on the tramp's jacket. 'It looks as though he could have been out when he was attacked. Drunk maybe.' The smell finally became too overwhelming and the DI stepped back out of the cubicle. However, he continued to study the carnage inside the small enclosure. 'There isn't much blood,' he observed. 'If he was stabbed it'd be everywhere. That wound in the throat would have cut his jugular vein. The whole place would be covered in blood.'

'Maybe he was killed somewhere else and dumped here,' Nicholson suggested.

'I think somebody would have noticed a person dragging a gutted body across Leicester Square. I mean, the place isn't exactly deserted at...' He paused a moment. 'What do you think was the time of death?'

'We won't know for sure until the lab boys have finished with him, but looking at the skin on the hands, it can't have been much later than eleven or so. Our bloke found him just after midnight and rigor mortis has only just started to set in.' Nicholson shrugged and took a long drag on his cigarette, blowing the smoke out in a long blue stream which momentarily masked the rank odours in the lavatory.

Grogan looked almost longingly at the haze of smoke and the cigarette, then stepped away from his colleague and gazed down at the glistening trail of slime across the floor. It was too thick to be saliva, he thought, and how come there was so much of it on the body, too? Grogan dug his hands into the pockets of his jacket and sighed. Usually upon reaching the scene of a crime he could glean at least two or three clues from what he saw. Possible murder weapon, sometimes even motive. But this body offered no such help. They didn't even know who the poor bastard was. The glamour of the police force, thought Grogan sardonically. Standing in a public toilet at one o'clock in the morning, surrounded by blood, piss and puke, staring into the trough of a urinal.

He brushed a hand through his tousled mop of greying hair and sighed heavily. Maybe the pieces would fit together better after the body had been examined by the lab boys. He certainly hoped so.

There was a flurry of movement from the top of the steps, and a moment later two ambulancemen descended, carrying a furled stretcher.

'In there,' said Grogan, hooking a thumb in the direction of the cubicle.

The stretcher was laid on the floor and one of the uniformed men entered the small enclosure. Grogan heard his low exclamation of revulsion as he saw the body. He turned to watch as the two men struggled to manoeuvre the corpse onto the waiting stretcher, one of them holding the spindly legs, the other hooking his arms beneath the shoulders of Tommy Price. They lifted carefully, but not carefully enough.

27

The body broke in half at the waist.

Grogan swallowed hard and turned to Nicholson as the two pieces were laid on the stretcher and covered with a blanket.

'Give me a cigarette,' said the DI as the ambulancemen passed close by with their grisly cargo.

'I thought you'd given up,' said Nicholson, as he watched his superior take an Embassy from the packet and light up.

'I had.'

Wednesday – the 12th

Four

The first thing which greeted Doctor Alan Finch as he entered the surgery was the strident ringing of the phone. He paused a moment, putting down his briefcase, but a second later the phone was answered by someone in reception. He heard a woman's voice and realized that the receptionist had already arrived. He should have realized it when he saw his mail and that of his two partners neatly laid out in separate piles. He smiled to himself as he reached for his own stack of white and brown envelopes.

There were a couple of circulars from drug companies, one offering a new tablet to aid in the relief of pre-menstrual tension, the other claiming that it had by far the most reliable new drug for controlling blood-pressure. Finch folded them both up and replaced them in their envelopes to read later. Then he opened the other mail. A blood test result confirmed his diagnosis that a particular patient was hypoglycaemic, and another told him that an exploratory operation to remove a growth from a middle-aged man's left lung had found the tumour to be benign. Finch smiled again.

He walked out into the reception, which was still empty of patients. A tall, heavily-built woman in her mid-thirties sat on the chair behind the reception desk, an appointment book open before her.

'Good morning, June,' Finch said, reaching for the pile of patients' notes which had been stacked carefully for him. 'Looks like being a busy day,' he added, indicating the notes.

'That's just for this morning, doctor,' June Webber told him. She stood up to retrieve a notepad which lay beside another phone. June was a big woman, almost five-ten, only an inch shorter than Finch himself. She had jet-black hair and an embarrassingly noticeable profusion of facial hair, particularly on her upper lip. But despite her physical shortcomings, she was a first-class worker and she, perhaps more than anyone else, had helped Finch to settle into this new practice which he'd been part of for just three months.

The surgery was a three-man collaboration in Bloomsbury Square and Finch, at thirty-two, was not only the newest partner, he was also the youngest. His colleagues were both only in their early forties but the age gap was sufficient to allow them some good-natured fun at the expense of the younger man. He took this in good humour because it made him feel a part of the set-up. He was 'the new boy' but the label was one which he didn't mind. He had found it surprisingly easy to settle in following the departure of his predecessor through ill health. Even that doctor's regular patients seemed to have taken to the newcomer, warming to his sincerity and concern. Such was the number of patients that each doctor was allocated just five minutes per patient, but people seldom left Finch's room in less than fifteen.

'You've got one or two calls to make before you see your first patient, doctor,' June told him, checking the notepad. 'There's one at a house in Clerkenwell.' She gave him the name and address. 'A woman is worried about her little boy. And there's another one at a flat in Flaxman Court, a Mrs Molly Foster. The notes are here.' She handed him two files which he read quickly.

'When's my first appointment in the surgery?' he asked.

'Ten thirty,' she told him.

'OK, I'll get going then.' Clutching the files, he made his way towards the rear entrance of the building. He crossed to his car, waving to one of his colleagues who had just pulled up nearby. Finch didn't wait to exchange greetings, but slid behind the wheel of the Chevette and started the engine. As he did so, he leant across and wound down the passenger-side window as well as his own. Although it was only 8.38 a.m., the sun was already climbing high into a clear blue sky. It promised to be another scorcher. Finch couldn't remember the last time it had rained, and on the news that morning he had heard talk of water rationing if the blazing weather continued. Already, parts of Britain were completely without water because reservoirs had dried up.

As he drove, the smell of petrol and diesel fumes filled the car, but Finch decided this was preferable to the unbearable heat he'd have to endure with the windows shut. He drove on, having decided to make the Clerkenwell call first. He flicked on the radio. Theresa had bought the radio and cassette player for him four years ago . . . He allowed the thought to trail off, trying to push any images of his wife from his mind. He turned up the volume and concentrated on weaving his way along streets which were still busy with commuters who insisted on the daily confrontations which driving to work brought. Finch was relieved that he didn't have too far to go.

'. . . who said that talks had broken down once more.' The newsreader's voice filled the car. 'Police in London today are trying to identify the remains of a man found in a public convenience in Leicester Square. The man had been badly mutilated but, as yet, his identity remains a mystery. Scotland Yard would not say if the man was murdered or not but they are treating his death as such . . .'

Finch eased the volume down again, turning the radio off as he swung the car into the street he was searching for. He double-checked the address on the sheet of paper beside him and drove the Chevette into a handy parking space.

It was 9.02.

Finch double-checked that his doors were locked before leaving the car. The sun was pouring heat down mercilessly now. The doctor wiped a bead of perspiration from his forehead with the corner of his handkerchief as he walked across the street towards the three-storey block of flats in Flaxman Court. The trip from Clerkenwell had taken him just under twenty-five minutes, not bad allowing for traffic. The call, he decided, had been necessary. The child, a boy of six, had been suffering from severely inflamed tonsils and a very bad cough. Finch had left a prescription and instructions that he was to be called again if there was no improvement within thirty-six hours. The boy's mother had been most grateful, the child himself a nice little chap. Not unlike his own son, Chris ...

Finch gritted his teeth, as if the memory was a painful one. With effort he succeeded in driving away the thoughts of his child. Temporarily at least.

He walked up to the first floor and found the flat he sought. Number five. Finch pressed the bell lightly and heard the two-tone chime inside. A moment later the door was opened and the doctor found himself confronted by a young woman he guessed to be in her late twenties. He settled on twenty-nine although her drawn expression perhaps added unfairly to her years. The dark rings beneath her eyes, he imagined, were the result of tears shed rather than sleepless nights. Otherwise, she was extraordinarily attractive, her small face framed by thick brown hair, high-lighted in places as if the sun were permanently shining on it. She looked at him with deep blue eyes which were at once welcoming and apprehensive.

'Doctor Finch?' she said, before he could speak.

He nodded, allowing himself to be ushered inside the flat.

It was light and airy, populated by dozens of house plants which stood like green sentinels all around the room. A particularly large rubber plant towered over the television set in one corner, its leaves brushing against a photo of the young woman who now led Finch towards a door to another room. He glanced quickly at the photo, which apparently had been taken recently. It showed the girl in some kind of uniform, but he couldn't make out what it was. Quite a contrast, however, to the flowing cheesecloth dress she wore now, the flared bottom reaching as far as her knees, revealing evenly tanned calves.

She motioned him into the next room where there were more plants, but smaller ones this time. It was a bedroom and he frowned as he caught sight of the occupant of the single bed.

'Could you leave us for a moment, Miss...'

'Foster,' she told him. 'Lisa Foster.'

He smiled, waited until she had left the room and then moved to the bed.

Finch laid his bag on a nearby dressing table and turned his full attention to the woman in the bed.

Her greying hair was pushed back from a sweat-stained forehead to reveal two large boils, one above the right eye, the other slightly higher. Both of the boils were badly swollen and looked on the point of bursting. On her sunken cheek there was another of the pustules, but this one was cracked and a thick yellowish fluid was dribbling slowly from it. There was another boil on her chin. Thick folds of flesh hung around her neck like a collar, and nestling in the hollow of her throat was another of the oozing sores.

'Mrs Foster,' said Finch, shaking the woman gently. 'Can you hear me?'

Molly Foster opened her eyes and looked at him with surprising alertness. There was a sparkle in those eyes which seemed to have deserted the rest of her body. She even managed a smile but, as she did, the boil on her chin opened slightly, releasing a thick purulent ooze. The smile dissolved into a wince of pain.

Finch took a tissue from a container in his pocket and wiped away the pus, then reached for his bag and removed a thermometer and stethoscope. He slipped the thermometer under Molly's tongue before easing down the sheets to expose her chest.

There were more lesions on her shoulders and breasts, one bulging and throbbing angrily like an extra nipple. Finch listened for the rhythmic thudding of her heart. It was normal. He checked the thermometer.

It too was normal. The mercury had not risen above the designated mark.

'How long have you been like this, Mrs Foster?' he asked, taking his opthalmoscope to peer into her eyes.

'Since last night,' she told him. 'Well, this morning really. I couldn't sleep, my daughter will tell you. Ever since my husband passed away I've had trouble sleeping. I got up at about four this morning to make myself a cup of tea.'

'Are you in pain?'

'Well, these,' she indicated one of the sores. 'They're painful, but otherwise no.'

He took the sphygmomanometer from his case and fastened the velcro strip around Molly's arm and then, using the small rubber pump, he began inflating the arm band to the correct pressure. Finch shook his head almost imperceptibly.

Her blood pressure was perfectly normal too.

'What's wrong with me, doctor?' she asked him.

Finch felt momentarily useless as he put his equipment away.

'Something which *I* can't discover with my simple methods,' he said, smiling. 'Do you have a phone I could use? I think you'd be better off in hospital, at least until we can find out what's caused those lesions. I'll call an ambulance.'

Molly nodded and watched him silently as he walked out of the room. He found Lisa sitting tensely on the edge of a chair. She stood up as he entered the room, the anxiety still on her face.

'What is it, doctor?' she asked.

'I don't know,' he said, somewhat apologetically. 'Some tests will need to be done. I have to call an ambulance.'

She showed him the phone and stood by as he dialled.

'Could it be an allergic reaction?' Lisa offered hopefully.

Finch shook his head.

'It's too extreme for that,' he told her. The phone at the other end was picked up and he gave the necessary information. The ambulance, he was told, would be there in twenty minutes.

'Perhaps you could pack some things for your mother,' Finch said. 'They may well want to keep her overnight.'

Lisa nodded.

'Which hospital?' she wanted to know.

'The Middlesex,' he said as she turned back towards the bedroom. 'Could you tell me where the bathroom is, please? I'd like to wash my hands.'

Lisa directed him, then she herself retreated from the room.

Finch filled the basin with warm water, scrubbed his hands twice, then rinsed them thoroughly. That done, he emptied the basin, ran some cold water and splashed his face with it in an effort to cool himself down. Moisture ran in rivulets down his face until he found a towel and dried himself, studying his reflection in the mirror above the sink for a moment. Molly Foster's condition certainly had him puzzled. Her heartbeat, temperature and blood pressure were all perfectly normal. Everything seemed to be normal except for the boils.

What the hell had caused them?

He replaced the towel and turned to leave the bathroom, noticing that in this room too there was greenery. A small rubber plant stood near the toilet.

What he didn't notice was the thick, glistening slime which criss-crossed the lower leaves.

Five

Some days the smell seemed stronger than others, and today it was particularly rank.

John Bateson coughed and waved a hand in front of his face but the smell of excrement swirled thickly around him like a dense cloud in the darkness of the sewer tunnel. The tunnel itself was over ten feet in diameter, with a ceiling high enough for a six-foot man to walk comfortably without stooping. As Bateson moved through the stream of dark fluid, it reached as high as his calves, but the thigh-length waders which he wore protected his legs from the evil-smelling water.

Somewhere ahead he could hear the steady dripping of

more water, and as he shone his torch upwards he saw that part of the brickwork about half-way up the side of the tunnel was cracked, several lumps of masonry having fallen into the effluent. Dark mould clung to the walls and ceiling of the tunnel, adding its own damp odour to the smell of excrement. Bateson held up his safety lamp, one eye on the red light, which as yet remained unlit. If it should glow even slightly, he and his companions would be forced to leave the sewer as this signalled a pocket of gas.

The water in the storm relief sewer was lower than usual because of the hot weather. It never rose much above five feet, unlike that in the large interceptor sewers. There, the level could reach seven or eight feet, completely filling the tunnels, especially in wet weather, but at the moment levels all over the system were down.

'You'd better check further on,' Harold Oldfield said, aiming his own torch deeper into the blackness. 'I'll take care of this break.'

Bateson nodded and splashed on down the tunnel, his torch beam moving back and forth ahead of him.

The constant flow of water had cut a deep swathe into the stonework near the water level. Bateson knelt to examine this more closely and prodded some of the eroded bricks. A lump of stone came away in his hand.

'This wall is going too,' he called to his colleague, his voice echoing in the silence of the tunnel.

'I'm going up to fetch the tools,' Oldfield called back. He turned and headed for the metal ladder, clambering up towards the manhole through which they'd both descended minutes earlier. The silence suddenly seemed to overwhelm Bateson. Alone in the tunnel he felt hemmed in by the solitude and gloom. The beam of his torch was powerful but he could see nothing outside its narrow width. There was a hazy shaft of light pouring in from the manhole above like some kind of ethereal shape in the blackness, but it was too far away to offer any comforting light.

Bateson had been a sewer engineer for just over two years, since he had left school, but still he had not managed to adjust to the sometimes claustrophobic conditions in which he worked. The darkness, the smell and the silence combined to make his work both uncomfortable and, more often than not, a little frightening. He had thought about leaving on numerous occasions but now, with his wife Karen expecting their first baby within the month, that was out of the question. He'd been lucky to get this job, and it was hardly the time to start looking for another one. He kept telling himself that he'd get used to it, but besides the sheer discomfort of wading around in other people's waste, there was an element of danger attached to the work. The sewers could flood, particularly after a heavy storm, with very little warning. He'd heard of men being swept to their deaths in torrents of water, and of others who had become lost in the maze of tunnels and had finally suffocated, died of fright or been gassed by the many pockets of lethal methane which collected below ground. And then there had been the stories of the rats. Oldfield and the other older men in his maintenance group had sworn that they'd seen rats as big as dogs in the tunnels. Bateson had dismissed their stories – giant rats existed only in horror films.

He heard a low rumbling sound, growing steadily louder, and it took him a second or two to realize that it was a Tube train passing below. Some of the sewers ran above the lines, others below them. Many were less than forty feet underground. The rumbling passed and the silence returned.

Somewhere behind him he heard a faint splash and he spun round, aiming his torch beam in the direction of the sound.

He could see nothing.

There was another splash, louder this time. Then another. Then silence again.

Bateson exhaled deeply. What the hell was the matter with him today? He administered a swift mental self-rebuke, trying to quell his unusually shaky nerves. He told himself that it was because he was worrying about Karen. Despite his insistence that he should stay at home with her (in case the baby was premature, he had argued), she had pushed him out to work. There was no way she was going to have the child yet, she assured him.

The thought of the birth did bring a momentary smile to his face. When the lad grew old enough he'd take him along to Stamford Bridge to watch Chelsea, dressed in his little blue-and-white scarf and hat. He'd make sure the little fellow didn't get into any bother. Bateson had many friends among the fraternity in The Shed and, besides, he knew how to handle himself. But once his son was with him things would be different. His son. The thought sent a swell of pride through him.

What if it was a girl? Shit, he hadn't though of that. He'd look a bit of a prick taking a girl to watch football, wouldn't he? He dismissed the idea. No, it was going to be a boy. No sweat.

Bateson's train of thought was suddenly broken by another loud splash, closer this time, and a second later something bumped against his boot.

He shone his torch down and saw that it was a turd.

The large black slug floated past unnoticed.

From the direction of the manhole there were sounds of activity, and a moment later Oldfield returned carrying a couple of tool bags, one of which he handed to his younger companion. Then he splashed back up the tunnel to get on with his own work. Both men set about their business.

'When's your old lady going to drop the foal then?' Oldfield called out. His voice reverberated eerily around the tunnel.

'Anytime now,' Bateson replied, reaching into his tool bag for a chisel.

'You're nervous, aren't you? It's easy to see. I was the same with my first one. My old lady was in labour for twelve hours, they thought she was going to die. But with the second and third, well, that was like shelling peas.' He chuckled loudly.

Bateson laughed too, the sound drowning out another series of splashes, each one closer to him than the last.

Five large slugs, each more than six inches in length, glided through the water with a grace unbefitting their bloated, obscene forms. They moved toward Bateson. Above him, clinging to the roof of the tunnel, dozens more slithered along, leaving their thick, reeking slime trails behind.

The first of those in the water reached Bateson's tool bag and crawled up onto it, hidden by the enveloping blackness.

'What are you going to call your youngster?' Oldfield enquired.

'I thought about Peter or David, maybe even Pat,' the younger man said, reaching into his bag for a hammer. He broke away some chipped brick and replaced the tool, his hand almost touching the second slug, which had now hauled itself inside.

Above, the other black abominations continued to draw closer.

'What if it's a girl?' Oldfield said, laughing.

Bateson thought for a moment then smiled broadly.

'Kerry,' he said, unhesitatingly. 'What do you reckon?'

Oldfield didn't answer.

'Harry, did you hear me?'

Still no answer.

'Harry, I...'

'I think we've got a problem,' Oldfield said, quietly, his eyes on the lights of his safety lamp.

The red warning light had begun to flicker rapidly, and now it glowed brilliant red.

'Gas,' he said hoarsely. 'Let's get out of here.'

Bateson was on his feet and starting to move when he felt something hit his back. He shuddered, wondering if a piece of mould had fallen from the roof of the tunnel.

Something else dropped onto him.

Something thick and wet. It was on his shoulder.

'Come on, move it, quick!' Oldfield called, already at the ladder which led up to the manhole.

Bateson brought his hand round and tried to brush the sticky lump from his overalls. In the darkness he was unable to see what it was. It felt cold and soft, like rancid faeces.

He grabbed his torch and swung it up, directing it at the roof above him, the light picking out the mass of slugs which seemed to be suspended there.

'Oh my God,' murmured Bateson, disgust in his voice.

41

As one, the slugs dropped from the roof.

Half a dozen latched onto his exposed face, fixing themselves to his flesh with their razor-sharp central teeth. Immediately the rasp-like radula teeth began slicing through skin and muscle as the slugs burrowed into Bateson's face. One of the monstrosities slipped into the welcoming wetness of his mouth, forcing its thick, swollen form down his throat and causing him to retch violently. But even the stream of vomit which spewed forth could not dislodge the slimy creature. Anchored by its central tooth, the slug remained where it was, eating into the back of its victim's throat.

Bateson clutched at the slugs on his face, tugging madly at one which was forcing its way into his left nostril.

Another slithered across his eye, driving its sickle-shaped main tooth into the tender tissue. Blood ran down his face in torrents, mingling with his vomit and the reeking slime exuded by the slugs.

Finally, close to unconsciousness, he toppled backwards into the stream of effluent, still tugging at the feeding beasts who were devouring his face. His groping fingers could not hold onto the slippery abominations and he writhed in helpless agony in the filthy water until, finally, one flailing hand touched something in the open toolbag.

He gripped the pliers and raised them to his face, fixing the jaws around the slug which had all but disappeared into his nostril. He only succeeded in snipping the tumescent form in half. A thick, reeking yellowish pus burst from the torn body, some of it spurting into his open mouth which was already filled with his own blood and the foul slime of the slug feeding inside his throat. He managed a loud gargling sound which echoed around the cavernous tunnel but then the slug detached itself, forcing its corpulent body even further until it blocked his windpipe.

Bateson thrashed about like an eel on a hot skillet, unable to breathe and wracked by agony such as he could never have imagined, yet still he fought back, using the pliers once more. He seized the head of another of the black creatures which was in the process of eating its way through his cheek. With a final defiant gesture, he snapped the pliers together, catching a large portion of his own skin between the blades. He pulled, his eyes bulging wide in unendurable pain. The slug came free but so did a sizeable strip of flesh. There was a sickening sound much like that of tearing material and the skin was ripped away like peeling wallpaper. A great, dripping flap of it hung from the pliers, which Bateson finally dropped. His body began to convulse madly, churning the filthy water around him into a froth.

Those slugs that had remained in the water moved swiftly towards the bloodied ruin which had once been his face, slithering and crawling over the bleeding lump.

Bateson felt as if his head were going to explode and now, as the slugs began eating into the flesh of his neck, he prayed for the end.

Moments before it came he felt more slugs dropping onto his body from the roof of the tunnel like a vile rain.

Then, mercifully, he felt nothing at all.

Harold Oldfield looked at his watch.

Over two minutes had passed since he had shouted his warning to Bateson, yet still the younger man had not emerged from the manhole. Finally, Oldfield fastened on his breathing apparatus and tested the flow of oxygen. He took another mask and cylinder from one of his colleagues and lowered himself back into the hole, climbing cautiously down the metal ladder. He paused halfway down and glanced at the warning beacon on his safety light.

As yet it had not lit up. Perhaps the pocket of gas had dispersed, Oldfield thought. He climbed the remaining few feet and lowered himself to the floor of the tunnel, glancing again at the warning light.

It flickered weakly but then went out completely.

Oldfield waited for long moments, then took his mask off.

'It's clear,' he shouted up at his colleagues who were peering down the shaft. Oldfield moved along the tunnel, his torch cutting a broad swath through the blackness.

'John,' he called.

Silence.

'John. Can you hear me?'

Still nothing.

Oldfield almost tripped over the tool bag.

He shone his torch down, over the area where Bateson had been working.

There was blood on the tool bag and something else too.

Something which glistened in the beam. A silvery fluid which dripped from the bag in thick globules. As he shone the torch around him he saw that the silvery secretion was on the walls and ceiling of the tunnel as well.

Of Bateson there was no sign.

Six

The clock in the reception area of the Middlesex Hospital showed that it was 7.21 p.m. Finch looked at his own watch and noticed that it had stopped. He decided to put it right later. He walked past the unattended desk near the main doors and strode towards a tall slim nurse who was helping a middle-aged man out of a wheelchair and onto a pair of crutches. Finch waited until she'd finished the delicate manoeuvre and then smiled warmly at her, happy to see the gesture returned.

'Could you check your record of admissions for today, please?' he asked. 'There's someone I'd like to see.'

The nurse made her way back to the reception desk, followed by the doctor.

'What was the name of the patient?' she asked, opening a large, bound tome on the desk.

'Foster. Molly Foster,' he told her. 'I'm her doctor. My

name is Finch.'

The girl ran one slender index finger down a column of names, jabbing at the one she sought.

'Mrs Foster is in Ward 5C, the lift is over there.' She pointed in the appropriate direction.

Finch thanked her, walked to the lift and punched the '5' button. The doors slid open promptly and he stepped in, leaning back against the rear wall of the car as it rose. His surgery had finished an hour earlier. He'd found the time to shower and drink a cup of tea before changing into an open-neck shirt and jeans. Then he'd driven to the hospital, determined to see if Molly Foster had made any progress, or at least to discover if the tests had yielded answers to the baffling questions he'd been confronted with earlier in the day. Finch couldn't help but wonder if he would always find time for individual patients, as he was doing now. In years to come, would he be unconcerned what became of them outside surgery hours? He knew that many doctors felt that way, but so far he had not been able to decide whether a detached attitude was unavoidable or essential, the product of over-work or of cynicism.

The lift bumped to a halt at the fifth floor and he stepped out.

There was a vending machine nearby, being fed coins by a youth in a leather jacket. A teenage girl, with her right leg in plaster, sat on the leather seat beside the machine and looked on as the lad pressed buttons and made a choice of drinks. The machine coughed out two cans of Coke and the couple talked animatedly as they drank.

The doctor glanced up at the sign above a set of swing doors which bore the legend 'Ward 5C'. He walked in, turning right, heading for the ward sister's desk. She was a small, slightly built woman in her thirties, a ladder in one stocking. Her face had a pinched look, made the worse by her long nose, but the harshness of her features was counter-balanced by the softness of her voice when she spoke.

'Can I help you, sir?' she said, in an accent with a slight Irish lilt.

Finch asked to see Molly Foster, told her why and waited to be shown to the appropriate bed. The duty sister accompanied him, indicating a set of screens which hid Molly from the view of the other patients. It was visiting time, so most patients had at least one friend or relative present and a low burble of conversation filled the ward. Finch approached the screens and moved them aside just enough to allow himself access.

Lisa Foster turned to look at him as she heard movement from behind her. She started to rise but Finch shook his head, looking first at her and then at her mother. Molly was asleep, her head turned to one side. The boils and sores had been dressed, and most of her face, neck and arms were now covered in bandages.

'I hope you don't mind me calling in,' Finch said. 'I thought I'd see how she was getting on.'

Lisa too had changed clothes since their first meeting. She now wore a light sweater, the baggy sleeves rolled up to her elbows. The folds of material largely concealed her small breasts but the tight jeans she wore accentuated the smoothe curve of her buttocks and the shapeliness of her thighs. Her hair looked as if it had been freshly washed for it gleamed beneath the lights. She wore only the merest hint of eye make-up.

'They gave her a sedative about an hour ago,' she told him. 'The ... boils were beginning to hurt her, she said.' Lisa looked away from Finch. 'I've been with her since they brought her in this morning.'

'You could do with a break,' he told her.

'I popped home for twenty minutes to change. I'm OK.'

Both of them turned as the screens were parted and a tall, raven-haired man in a white coat entered. He looked at Finch and Lisa over the top of his glasses, then picked up the board which hung from the bottom of Molly's bed.

Finch introduced himself and said, 'I'm the doctor who asked for Mrs Foster's admission.'

The other man nodded.

'Have you any idea what the problem might be?' Finch

46

asked.

'Not yet.' The man looked at Lisa and smiled thinly. 'Would you step outside for a moment, Miss Foster?'

Lisa looked concerned.

'Is anything wrong?' she said.

'You'll be told everything we know, but not until we know it,' the man in the white coat said, then remained quiet until Lisa was out of earshot. Then he looked at Finch. 'My name's Benton. Peter Benton. I'm in charge of the tests we're running on Mrs Foster.' He sighed. 'I'm afraid her condition has deteriorated since she was admitted.' He stepped to the bed and lifted one of Molly's arms, carefully unwrapping a dressing beneath her elbow. He removed the gauze pad which covered the affected area.

The boil looked on the point of bursting, a liquescent nodule seeping pus from its edges, but it was the area around the boil which Benton indicated. It looked yellow beneath the bright lights, the veins standing out darkly against the wasted skin.

'The infection's spreading,' Finch said flatly, recognizing the symptom.

'Her temperature has risen in the last two hours, and so has her blood pressure,' Benton informed him. 'She was in so much pain we had to sedate her.'

'What have the tests revealed?'

'We're still waiting for the results. We took blood samples, skin sections and tissue from the pustules themselves. We haven't tried any medication yet, not until we know what we're dealing with.' He carefully re-bandaged the sore. 'The next step is to remove one of the lesions and examine it.'

Finch nodded and turned to leave.

'I'll be in touch,' he said.

'Could you have a word with her daughter?' asked Benton. 'Try to persuade her there's nothing she can do? I've tried but...' He shrugged and let the sentence trail off. 'She'd be better off at home.'

'I'll see what I can do,' Finch promised and walked back up the ward.

He found Lisa sitting by the window looking out at the sun, which had finally lost its earlier intensity and was sinking slowly toward the tall buildings of London's skyline. Now reduced to a glowing orange disk in the gathering evening haze, its soft warmth was a welcome relief from the fierce mid-day heat.

Finch paused for a moment, studying Lisa's profile as she gazed out of the window, then he coughed loudly and theatrically. She turned, getting to her feet.

'Can I go back in now?' she asked him.

'Your mother will be out for quite a while yet,' he said. 'Sitting staring at her isn't going to do either of you any good.' He raised his eyebrows.

Lisa nodded.

'Can I buy you a cup of coffee?' he asked, smiling, moving towards the vending machine.

She nodded and followed him, standing nearby as he pushed the coins in and then jabbed the buttons. The machine dropped a cup obligingly, but proceeded to fill it with nothing more than hot water.

'Do you take sugar in your water?' he asked, with a grin.

Lisa looked at him blankly for a moment, and then, for the first time since he'd met her, she too smiled.

'Perhaps we'd be better off in the canteen,' Finch suggested.

They walked to the lift.

Seven

Lisa cradled the coffee cup in her hand, looking down into the swirling brown liquid which she had just stirred for the third time.

Finch sipped his own drink and looked at her as if waiting for some word or reaction.

The hospital canteen was filled with patients, visitors, doctors, nurses and other staff, all drinking coffee or eating sandwiches. A steady babble of conversation filled the room.

'To use a time-honoured medical cliché,' said Finch, his eyes never leaving Lisa, 'worrying about your mother won't help either of you. There's nothing you can do here at the moment.'

'That's what Doctor Benton told me,' she admitted. 'He suggested that I go home and wait until they contact me.'

'That's very good advice.'

'Doctors stick together, don't they?' she said sardonically.

'Listen, Miss Foster, no one's saying you don't have a right to be worried but if you carry on this way you'll be exhausted and no help to your mother when she needs you.'

'Are you persuading me or patronizing me, doctor?' There was a slight edge to her voice which Finch was not slow to pick up. He saw a momentary iciness in her blue eyes, but it rapidly melted. 'I'm sorry,' she sighed. 'I didn't mean that. I know you're considering *my* health as well.' She took a sip of her coffee. 'By the way, it was thoughtful of you to come and see my mother. Thank you.'

'A doctor's duties shouldn't end when his surgery closes, Miss Foster.'

'Lisa,' she told him. 'Please call me Lisa.'

Finch smiled, and was pleased to see her return the gesture.

'Have the rest of your family been told about this?' he enquired.

'I didn't see any reason, doctor,' she told him.

'Alan,' he said. 'My name is Alan. Doctors have first names too.'

She smiled again, the gesture lighting her face.

'Alan,' she repeated. 'No, I haven't told any of my family about what's happened because there wouldn't be much point. I'm the only one who sees Mother from one week to the next. If I hadn't called in today she'd have stayed the way she was. On her own with no one to help her.'

'I didn't mean to pry,' Finch said, almost apologetically. She dismissed his words.

'Why should I keep it a secret? I've got two sisters and two brothers and if Mother sees any of them more than twice in a year, then she's lucky. One of them will phone occasionally if they've got nothing else to do but apart from that I'm the only one who calls in on her. I sometimes stop there at weekends.'

Finch looked briefly at her hands and saw that there was no sign of a wedding or engagement ring.

'She's got two three-year old grandchildren that she's never even seen,' Lisa continued, as if anxious to relieve herself of some kind of burden. The bitterness in her voice was unsettling. 'That's the way it's been for as long as I can remember. I've always been the one who looked after her when she needed help, and God knows I owe it to her.'

'What about your father?' Finch enquired.

'He died when I was fifteen. My mother worshipped him. After his death she was never the same. She never stopped loving him, she never will. I often wonder what it must be like to feel that way about someone.' She took a sip of coffee, lowering her eyes momentarily as if she had opened up just a little more than she wanted to.

'Up until today, though, your mother's been a fit woman, hasn't she?' Finch said. 'I checked back through the records.'

Lisa nodded.

'And you've no idea at all what might have caused this . . .' He allowed the sentence to trail off.

'She phoned me this morning about six and asked me to call in on her. When I got there that was how I found her.'

'Where do you live?' he wanted to know.

'I'm a receptionist at the Strand Palace Hotel, I've got a room there. The wages aren't too great but at least the food and lodging are free.' She smiled humourlessly. 'But I'm staying at my mother's place until all this is sorted out. I was due a few days' holiday. The management are pretty good about things like that.' She finished her coffee and pushed the cup away. Finch watched as she ran both hands through her thick hair and shook her head, causing the silken cascade to shimmer beneath the lights.

'Well, you know the *interesting* things about me,' she said, mockingly, 'but I don't know anything about you. Can you tell me or is it breaking the Hippocratic Oath?' She smiled.

'What do you want to know?' he asked.

'How long have you been a doctor?'

'I studied medicine until I was twenty-eight. When I finished I joined a National Health practice in Camden Town for a year, then I moved to another in Notting Hill, full time, up until three months ago. I've been with this private practice since then.'

'Are you married?'

'Divorced,' he said, his tone softening.

'I'm sorry. Still, at least you've had your chance. I sometimes wonder if I'm going to end up on the shelf. Twenty-eight and still single. Even my mum has been telling me it was time I settled down.'

'I don't think there's much chance of *you* ending up on the shelf. You're a very attractive young woman.'

Lisa smiled self-consciously and attempted to change the subject.

'You obviously enjoy your work,' she said to him.

'Yes, I do. But it has its moments of pain too.' His voice took on a reflective note. 'Trying to tell a young couple that their ten-month-old son is dying of leukaemia isn't easy. I sometimes admire other doctors who are able to cut themselves off from their patients, at least on an emotional level. I'm afraid I haven't been able to do that. Not yet anyway.'

Lisa ran an appraising eye over him, studying his face. His hair was dark, almost black, and although he was clean shaven, the skin around his cheeks and chin also looked dark, as if his whiskers defied even the sharpest razor. His forehead was deeply lined, his eyes framed by thick eyebrows and high cheekbones. She looked at his hands, clasped on the table before him, and sensed a gentleness in them, despite their size. His forearms were thick and heavily muscled, clearly visible as his sleeves were rolled up.

He noticed her looking at him. Their eyes met and they held each other's gaze for fleeting moments.

'You look tired,' Finch told her.

'I'm all right,' she reassured him. 'I think it's time I got back up to the ward.'

'Lisa, Doctor Benton was right. There's nothing you can do there.'

'I can't bear to think of my mother here, alone.'

'She's being well cared for. Now, will you let me drive you home? My car's outside.'

She hesitated and inhaled deeply, letting out the breath in a long sigh.

'All right. I suppose there *is* nothing I can do,' she admitted reluctantly. 'I'd appreciate it if you'd take me home.' They both rose and walked slowly from the canteen, through reception and out into the dusk. The sun had just sunk out of sight and a slight breeze had sprung up. Lisa rolled down the sleeves of her sweater while she waited for Finch to unlock the Chevette. She slid into the passenger seat and he settled himself behind the wheel a moment later, adjusting his rear view mirror before starting the car.

As he guided it out into the traffic an ambulance passed them, its lights spinning silently. Finch glanced behind him and saw two uniformed men hurrying from the vehicle carrying a stretcher and its load. They disappeared through the doors marked 'Casualty'.

Neither he nor Lisa spoke.

The doctor drove steadily, in no hurry to reach his destination, and Lisa seemed quite content to gaze abstractedly out of the window as the Chevette threaded its way through the cars and lorries, bikes and vans which dotted the streets leading away from the hospital.

'You said you were divorced,' she said, quite unexpectedly. 'How long had you been married? If you don't mind me asking?'

He shook his head.

'Six years,' he told her.

'Any children?'

Finch was silent for a moment and Lisa looked across at him, studying his profile. She was about to repeat her question when he answered.

'One. A boy. We had him soon after we were married.' He smiled but there was no warmth in it. 'Even doctors make mistakes occasionally, you know.'

Lisa realized that she had touched on a delicate point and she dropped the subject, her own problems now drifting back into her mind.

'Do you think my mother is going to die?' she asked him suddenly.

Finch frowned.

'No,' he said, softly, and once more their eyes briefly locked.

They drove the rest of the way in silence until he eventually pulled up outside the flats in Flaxman Court.

'Thank you,' said Lisa, reaching for the door handle. 'You've been very kind.' She flashed him that radiant smile once more. 'Perhaps I'll see you again.'

'I'm sure you will,' he replied. 'Though hopefully under happier circumstances.'

They exchanged brief farewells and she climbed out of the car. Finch watched as she walked quickly to the flats, not looking back. He exhaled deeply. Should he have told her that the infection was spreading?

No, leave it to the hospital, he told himself.

As he started the car he wondered about Lisa's question. *Was* her mother going to die?

He wished he knew.

Finch drove off, the cool wind through the open window making him shiver.

Eight

In the growing darkness, the waters of the Thames looked black. The river curved through the city like a huge bloated tongue. The current heat wave had taken its toll even on the mighty river and the water level was down a good two feet. The banks on either side were clearly visible, sloping down at a sharp angle to the murky water. Normally hidden by the constant flow, they were now revealed as dirty stretches of shale and mud, baked hard in places by the day's unrelenting heat. A faintly rancid smell hung over the water, drifting ashore every so often when propelled by the gathering evening breezes.

Lights on the embankment high above, and on the parapets of Westminster Bridge, were reflected in the surface of the river like jewels in a dirty mirror.

'You know, we must want our bleeding heads tested,' said Ralph Patterson, trying to force a maggot onto his hook.

'I'm telling you, Ralph,' Trevor Doyle insisted. 'Some geezer told me he'd heard that there were trout in the Thames again.'

'All that's in the Thames is a few hundred tons of junk and some extra shit from these bleeding sewer outlets.' Patterson turned and looked at the yawning mouth of the pipe behind him. It emerged from the wall of the embankment like a hungry worm, a vile smell wafting from the black maw. Normally the pipes were covered but the drop in the water level had exposed them.

'Trout feed on human waste and that,' Doyle insisted. 'There's bound to be more of them around here. It stands to reason. I bet you we catch one.'

He cast his line into the black waters and stood contentedly.

'All we're going to catch is a roasting off the law,' Patterson told him. 'I'm sure this isn't legal.'

Doyle ignored him and re-adjusted his line.

Both men were in their late twenties, Patterson slightly older. He had the collar of his denim jacket pulled up to protect his neck from the cold breeze which was blowing along the embankment.

Doyle wore only a short-sleeved sweatshirt and the flesh on his arms had already risen into goose-pimples.

'I hope the tide doesn't come in,' he said, shivering.

Patterson looked at him and shook his head, but his frown dissolved into a look of surprise as he felt his rod buck in his hand.

'Sod me, I reckon I've got something,' he said in amazement. He began reeling in, tugging hard to coax his catch free of the water. The rod was bending from what was obviously a considerable weight on the other end and Doyle stood by, mesmerised, as his companion continued to wrestle with whatever he'd hooked.

'Well, don't just stand there,' Patterson said. 'Get hold of the bloody rod and help me pull.'

'I told you, didn't I?' Doyle said, grinning. 'You wouldn't believe me, would you?'

Both men gave a final mighty heave and an object cleared the water, flew through the air and landed with a thud close to them. They both spun round to look at it.

'And how do you suggest we cook *that*?' said Patterson, irritably.

He prodded the wooden toilet seat with the toe of his trainer and glared at his companion.

'Someone must have chucked it over the side of a ship,' Doyle said. 'Well, it would have been asking too much to get a fish straight off, wouldn't it?'

Patterson didn't answer. He was busy pushing another maggot onto his hook.

'You know, we'd have more chance of catching a trout in

Trafalgar Square fountains,' he said, casting his line once more into the murky river.

'All we've got to do is wait,' Doyle assured him.

'We could have been sitting in the pub, you know. I'm giving it half an hour, tops, then I'm off. You can stand here all night if you want to.'

'Ralph, you know your trouble? You've got no spirit of adventure,' said Doyle.

Five minutes passed.

Ten.

Doyle was starting to feel colder.

'Lend us your jacket for a minute,' he said, shivering.

'Piss off,' Patterson said. 'You wanted to come fishing, you put up with the weather.'

'Oh come on, Ralph, you've got a sweater on under there.'

'Keep fishing and shut up,' Patterson said, chuckling.

Another five minutes and Doyle put down his rod.

'Where the hell are you going?' his friend asked.

'I'm going to shelter inside that bloody pipe for a minute,' he said, motioning towards the sewer outlet. 'I'm freezing to death.' He walked the five or six yards to the mouth of the culvert and climbed in, glad to be out of the chill breeze for a moment. Perhaps Ralph was right. Maybe there weren't any trout in the Thames. He muttered to himself. He'd hammer the bastard who'd told him there were. Doyle rubbed his arms and stamped his feet in an attempt to restore some warmth to his limbs. He wrinkled his nose at a particularly vile stench which seemed to be coming from just inside the pipe. It was like bad meat. He recognized the smell because he'd once worked in the freezer room of a meat factory, humping the carcasses. One day the fridges had blown out and every single piece of meat had gone off. The stench had been unbelievable.

And now he was smelling it again.

Doyle turned, peering into the forbidding blackness of the tunnel. However, there was enough light to illuminate the first six or seven feet of the large pipe.

The body was sprawled in an unearthly position, one arm

stretched out in front of it, the other bent and twisted behind the back. Both legs were tucked up to what remained of the chest, as if the corpse were kneeling. Its face was pressed to the floor of the culvert, away from Doyle's view.

'Jesus Christ,' he murmured, crouching low, covering his nose against the choking stench. He reached out one shaking hand and touched the outstretched arm.

Even that was enough to cause the body to topple over and Doyle found himself staring into what had once been a face. The flesh had been stripped from it as cleanly as if someone had gone over it with a blow torch, removing every last shred of skin. There were several loose flaps around the neck, which was holed in numerous places as if it had been punctured. The mouth hung open in a silent scream.

'Ralph,' he shrieked, his eyes riveted to the body, staring in horror at gleaming bones and the tattered remains of skin which still clung to the outstretched hand. He shouted Patterson's name again.

'Come here, quick,' he bellowed.

Patterson dropped his rod and sprinted over to where his friend stood gaping at the corpse. The smell hit him like an invisible fist and he covered his face with one hand.

'Fucking hell,' he mumbled, trying not to vomit, but his stomach kept turning violent somersaults as he studied the body. It was clad in overalls, torn and holed in several places, especially around the chest. Those empty, sightless eye sockets fixed him in an unseeing stare, and finally he turned away, gulping down great lungfuls of air.

'We'd better get the law,' said Doyle, backing off. 'Come on.'

Patterson needed no prompting. Both men turned and ran, but as he moved away from the monstrous vision which lay in the pipe, Doyle noticed something.

On the third finger of the left hand, the digit now fleshless and broken, a wedding ring glinted.

Six or seven arc lamps had been set up around the entrance to the sewer outlet, their blinding iridescence causing Detective

Inspector Grogan to wince as he made his way towards the opening. Two or three forensics men were already on the scene, one on his hands and knees near the pipe scrabbling around in the muck and stones. There was another light hanging inside the pipe, illuminating the remains of the corpse. Grogan wrinkled his nose as he climbed in.

Detective Sergeant Nicholson and a uniformed man were standing over the twisted remains.

'Who is he?' asked Grogan, nodding down at the body.

'His name's John Bateson,' the DS said. 'He was reported missing this afternoon by a couple of his workmates. It seems they were working in a storm relief sewer just off the Haymarket. The others cleared out because there was a gas leak. When one of them went back down there was no sign of Bateson.'

'So his body was swept here by the water in the sewers?' Grogan asked.

Nicholson nodded.

'What the hell happened to his face?' the DI pondered aloud. 'It looks like the same kind of damage we found on that poor sod in Leicester Square.'

Nicholson stooped and unfastened the dead man's overalls, pulling them open.

The entire chest and stomach cavity had been removed. Only shreds of mottled flesh and cracked bone remained beneath the overalls.

Grogan sighed, looking down at the wedding ring on the finger of the corpse.

'Someone had better tell his wife,' he murmured. Then, turning to leave, he looked back at Nicholson.

'I want the pathologist's reports on both victims as soon as possible. Let's see what he makes of it.'

The smell of death hung heavily in he air.

Nine

Finch juggled the cartons of Chinese food in both arms as he entered the kitchen, nudging the light on with one elbow. He winced as he felt hot barbecue sauce dripping through a rent in one of the cardboard containers onto his hand. The doctor dumped his supper on the table and wiped his hands on a towel. Ironically for a man who spent a good deal of his working life extolling the values of a balanced diet, Finch was a junk-food fanatic. Chinese or Indian, Macdonalds or just plain fish and chips, he was never averse to a take-away meal even though it might be lacking in nutrition. He found himself a knife and fork, then went and retrieved the evening paper from the front-door letterbox before sitting down at the table to eat straight from the cartons.

The house seemed strangely unwelcoming and silent, and Finch felt as if he were intruding upon the solitude. He ate slowly, pushing each carton aside when it was empty. As usual, he managed to time his last mouthful perfectly to match his completion of the paper. Then he got to his feet and stuffed the food containers and newspaper into the waste bin. The doctor wandered into the sitting room and flicked on the standard lamp. Again the silence seemed to swallow him up and he switched on the television. It at least provided the illusion of company.

The house in Westbourne Terrace was large, too large for one person, Finch had decided, and he'd been toying with the idea of selling it and moving into something smaller. A flat, ideally. Now that he was on his own the extra space was unnecessary.

On his own.

The thought drifted around in his mind as he sat down facing the television, looking at the picture but not really seeing anything.

He had lived alone for almost two years, ever since the break-up of his marriage. The split between Theresa and himself had been an ugly one and, at least on her part, the hostility had not ended with the separation. Their relationship had always been stormy, due in part to their very definite views on how they each wanted their careers to progress. Both possessed a single mindedness which bordered on obsession. His to become a doctor. Hers to take over the position of editor on the fashion magazine she worked for. Theresa was impulsive, quick-tempered, and when the need arose, ruthless. She was also stunningly attractive. A tall, statuesque woman with flowing auburn hair and a voice pitched so low that the word husky might well have been invented to describe it. She smouldered with an understated sensuality which many men found irresistible. Unfortunately for Finch, Theresa was not noted for her fidelity. Twice while they were engaged she had indulged in petty affairs, on each occasion with someone from the magazine where she worked. Quite how they came to be married sometimes seemed a mystery to Finch. But, at the beginning, things had run smoothly enough. Until she had discovered she was pregnant.

At that time he had discovered a curious ambivalence in her character. She knew that the birth of a child would wreck her chances of becoming editor of the magazine and yet she refused an abortion. The full weight of her anger and disappointment was directed at Finch. She blamed him for her pregnancy. Despite the fact that she had been taking the contraceptive pill for four years it had still happened. Finch himself ascribed the mishap to the fact that she had been suffering from a virus around the time she fell pregnant. It would have been quite easy for her to have vomited up the pill.

He understood her anger and disappointment but something nagged at the back of his mind. It had done at the time and it still did. Theresa had been involved with an advertising executive at the magazine, and Finch harboured suspicions that the child was the secret offspring of the other man. This had never been proved, or even discussed by himself and Theresa, but the fact that since she had left Finch she'd been living with that same man seemed to substantiate his fears. Nevertheless, when the child, a boy, had been born, both he and Theresa had shown it more love than any child could have expected under the circumstances. Theresa was a wonderful mother, but she had still felt an antagonism towards Finch which as time progressed had fermented into open dislike and resentment. He had his career, after all. It was she who had sacrificed everything.

The divorce had been almost inevitable and Finch, despite the fact that he loved his son, did not contest custody. He knew that Theresa and her lover could provide a better home. The doctor had to be content with his twice-monthly visits. He reached for the letter which lay on the coffee table beside his chair and opened it, re-reading the brief note which had arrived that morning. It was written in Theresa's distinctive sweeping script:

> *Dear Alan,*
> *You can pick Christopher up at noon this Sunday. I'll meet you outside the main entrance of Regents Park. If I'm not there then Richard will be. Have Christopher back at my place by seven.*
> *Theresa.*

He replaced the letter on the table and sat back in the chair, rubbing both hands over his face. The television flickered before him, a programme about the actress Meryl Streep. She was talking about her role in the film *Kramer Versus Kramer*, particularly the scene in which she was in court fighting for the custody of her son and . . .

Finch switched it off.

Thursday – the 13th

Ten

George Bennett stood gazing out of the window, enjoying the feel of the sun on his skin. The heatwave showed no sign of letting up and London, indeed the entire country, once more faced the prospect of baking in the unrelenting heat. The long-term forecast offered no respite. The air conditioning inside the office was turned on full but the room was still like a greenhouse.

Bennett took another sunflower seed from the small bag which he held and popped it into his mouth. He'd been up since six that morning. He'd reported in to Scotland Yard at eight-thirty, changed out of his track-suit into more suitable attire and set to work. Bennett had jogged to work from his home in Upper Norwood for the last eight months. That regular exercise combined with his carefully-prepared diet, he was convinced, had made him a healthier person. He had, over the last week or so, managed to persuade his wife to give up all red meat and other cholesterol-rich foods. The next step was to coax her into the programme of exercises which he'd devised for her. He himself visited the local leisure centre at least three times a week to work out with weights and tone up his body. After so long abusing it, Bennett was at last beginning to feel the benefits of his regime. Not only did it make him feel better physically, it also sharpened his mental abilities, and the meditative part of his work-out enabled him to blot out the sights and sounds of his day's labour.

He felt that this was essential, owing to the nature of that work.

He'd been a pathologist for nearly twenty-two years,

twelve of those at Scotland Yard. There wasn't much that escaped his keen eyes and mind, but at the moment he was worried. His face, perpetually round and flabby despite the exercises, did not carry its usual look of casual humour. Lines creased his forehead as he continued looking out onto the sun-drenched city.

Behind him, seated at his desk, Detective Inspector Ray Grogan scanned the two reports once more, then sat back in his chair, wiping a thin film of perspiration from his forehead. He hated the heat. The DI loosened his tie slightly and took a sip of his coffee, which he found to his distaste had gone cold.

'So the wounds on both bodies weren't made with knives?' he said.

Bennett walked around to the front of the desk, popping another sunflower seed into his mouth. He shook his head.

'X-rays on both Bateson and the tramp showed no evidence of metal fragments anywhere on the body. Besides, the edges of the wounds were ragged, especially those in the chest and abdomen. A blade would have left a cleaner cut. Also there was no scoring on any of the bones. I expected it on the faces, I mean, they'd been almost completely removed, if that's the right word. As if someone had peeled them off, piece by piece.'

Grogan nodded.

'I know, I saw them. Remember?' he said, sardonically. Then, referring to the reports once more, 'You've got Bateson's weight as five stone four pounds. He was over five feet ten, he should have weighed at least twelve stone.'

'There was so much tissue loss,' Bennett explained. 'Don't forget, in both cases, the thorax was empty of organs. The liver, intestines and lungs alone make up a large proportion of the body weight. And besides that, the flesh had been stripped to the bone from the legs and arms, in fact over most of the body.'

'So the manner of death in both cases is identical. And yet there's no conceivable link between the two victims. A tramp and a happily married man about to become a father.' Grogan tapped the desk agitatedly. 'What the hell do they have in common?' He sighed and reached for his cigarettes.

'You should smoke low-tar if you *have* to smoke,' Bennett told him.

'Yeah, I know,' Grogan said. 'I should also change my socks twice a day and not moan about my old lady's cooking.' He sucked hard on the fag, blowing out a long stream of blue smoke. 'I'll tell you what puzzles me. Bateson was down the sewer when he was killed and three of his mates were close by. How did the murderer get to him?'

The question went unanswered and silence descended for a moment, finally broken again by Grogan.

'If it wasn't a metal blade that inflicted the injuries,' he began, 'could it have been a synthetic weapon of some kind? Very hard plastic maybe?'

'No. Traces of any other substance would have showed up on the ultra-violet scan I did.'

'You're a great help, George,' Grogan told him, raising his eyebrows. 'Could it be two different murderers? We're only assuming the killings are linked.'

'With exactly the same MO? You know better than that, Ray.'

'Indulge me, you bastard, I was playing that much maligned game affectionately known as clutching at straws.' The smile faded rapidly from the DI's face, to be replaced by a look of angry bewilderment. 'In both cases the flesh was stripped away and the internal organs removed, so why haven't we found any trace of them? They weren't taken from the scene of the crime in the first place, or we'd have found fragments, or at least blood leading out of the toilet. What the bloody hell happened to them?'

Bennett continued munching his sunflower seeds, a thought flickering behind his eyes.

'It could be some kind of animal,' he ventured.

Grogan raised his eyebrows.

'Just an idea,' the pathologist said, almost apologetically.

'Well, that's all we've got, isn't it? Ideas?' Grogan said, wearily. 'Two corpses, a few ideas but not one fucking lead.' He ground out his cigarette angrily and watched the plume of smoke rise mournfully into the air.

Eleven

The dog was a cross-breed, part Alsatian, part Collie, retaining the elegance of the latter and the sleek build of the former. It padded slowly up the street, the pavement uncomfortably hot beneath its paws. Every now and then it would stop and prick up its ears as a car or motor-bike passed, sometimes barking at the offending machine. For the hot weather made the dog listless and irritable. It moved past people without a sound, however, for it had no hatred of man. The dog had always been treated well by its owners.

It paused for a moment to lap at the spilled contents of a Coke can which lay in the gutter, the fizzy liquid slaking its thirst at least for the moment. What the dog really sought was shade, somewhere to shelter from the merciless blanket of heat which lay over the city like a stifling shroud. High above, the vapour trails of aeroplanes criss-crossed the canopy of blue like chalk-marks on a blackboard.

The dog rounded a corner, tongue hanging from its mouth. Up ahead it saw what it sought. It moved on without increasing its pace, passing the odd parked car. It had tried crawling beneath one of the machines before but the smell of petrol had driven it away. Now it approached the empty building, the black gap in the boarded-up window beckoning it. The dog was barely able to squeeze through the opening between the planks but, panting heavily, it finally succeeded in hauling its sleek form into the murky, welcoming coolness.

The dog sniffed the stagnant air, detecting the smell of decay and filth, but also something more potent. A pungent odour which, simultaneously, both repelled and attracted it.

The building had once housed a small delicatessen. The empty shelves were now thick with dust and ancient cobwebs where large spiders lay in wait for the dozens of flies which buzzed lazily around the abandoned building.

To the rear was a small kitchen area, used by staff when the shop had been open, and it was towards this that the dog headed, drawn by the strange smell it had detected on entering the building.

The sink had been removed and only a hole in the ground remained where the pipe had once been.

Around this pipe were several trails of slime, thick and glutinous, cutting through the dust on the floor like tears down a dirt encrusted cheek.

The dog licked at one of the slime trails, shaking its head and growling as it tasted the vile substance. It tried to remove the sticky fluid from its tongue by scraping it with one dusty paw but this didn't seem to work. The dog made a retching sound, but seconds later it seemed to forget the foul taste. Its ears pricked up and it stood motionless, watching the top of the pipe.

The first slug, seven inches long and as thick as a man's index finger, slithered from the pipe.

It was followed by a second. And a third.

The dog didn't move.

Mark Franklin had been following the dog for nearly fifteen minutes, and more than once he thought he'd lost track of it. His mother had told him that Prince liked to roam the streets and Mark had decided to use his dog's habit for his own amusement. He'd let Prince out, given him thirty seconds start, then followed him just like they did in 'The Professionals'. They called it 'putting a tail on the suspect'. He chuckled to himself. Not hard to do as Prince already had a tail. Mark turned the corner just in time to see it disappearing as his dog slipped through the gap in the front of the empty shop.

He pulled the plastic radio from his belt, and without

taking his eyes off the shopfront, he spoke into it:

'This is Bodie calling Cowley. Suspect cornered. Will take action now. Over and out.'

He replaced the radio and took a model .45 automatic from the plastic shoulder holster which he wore, then made his way slowly down the street towards the building.

There was a sudden movement off to his right and he spun round.

Two children, younger than himself, were emerging from a small newsagents' clutching ice-creams. Mark decided that the suspect could wait until he'd bought himself a Mini Milk. He put his plastic gun away and rummaged in the pocket of his jeans for some money.

It was cool inside the shop and he stood beside the fridge, enjoying the cold air which wafted up from the freezer. Finally he reached in and selected a lolly, joining the small queue to pay for it.

Mark was eleven. He was happy playing on his own. Other children in the area didn't bother with him much, and even at school he had not yet found a group of friends who would share their time with him. His mother had worried at first, but Mark did not seem to care. He was more than able to amuse himself during the long summer holidays, something for which his mother was grateful because she had a cleaning job in a West End cinema and couldn't stay at home to keep Mark entertained.

He was a slightly built lad. His short hair gleamed in the sunlight, brushed back from a high forehead which already bore one or two small spots – a portent of the onslaught of acne which would no doubt plague him in his teenage years. He wore a brilliant white T-shirt with 'L.A. RAIDERS' on it in large red letters (a present brought back from the States by his grandparents), and a pair of brown cords which were a little too long and concertinaed around the tops of his trainers.

Mark leant against the wall of the newsagents' and slurped away at his Mini Milk. The suspect could wait until he'd finished.

The slugs oozed out of the pipe like a treacly river of oil, spilling onto the dusty floor of the abandoned shop. The largest ones moved towards the dog, which still sat motionless, watching intently. Finally, when the closest was less than a foot way, Prince ducked his head close to the slug and sniffed the black creature, which immediately retracted its eye stalks and stopped moving. Those around it, however, did not.

The dog licked one of the others, again growling at the vile taste of the mucus covering which sheathed its fat body.

The slug bit into the dog's tongue and hung there, suspended by its central tooth, as if attempting to pull the tender strip of muscle from its root.

Prince tried to yelp but only succeeded in making a high pitched whine deep in his throat. He shook his head, retracting his tongue and grinding the bloated slug between his powerful jaws. A mixture of blood and mucoid pus dripped to the floor in thick dollops.

Two more of the larger slugs fastened themselves to one of the dog's forepaws and began burrowing into the flesh. Prince snapped at them but could not dislodge them, and now more slugs were slithering up his other front leg, burrowing deep into skin and muscle.

He fell forward, and in that split second five or six more of the black monstrosities were able to grip his side. He snapped at another, pulping it between his teeth, heaving at the disgusting taste. Blood jetted from his wounds and sprayed across the dusty floor.

One of the largest slugs slithered up the dog's back, resisting all attempts to dislodge it until finally it reached the exposed ear. The monstrous creature fixed its mouth parts firmly inside Prince's ear and began feeding, boring deeper. Towards the brain.

The dog at last tried to run but the sheer weight of his attackers slowed his flight and he could only crawl as more and more slugs found their way onto his body and set to work with their teeth, sucking his warm blood which filled their bodies, pumping them up like leeches until it seemed they would burst.

And still the dog tried to crawl away, leaving a trail of blood and slime.

Even when his front legs had been eaten to the bone he kept trying to escape.

From the pipe in the floor yet more slugs emerged. A never-ending black torrent of death.

Mark finished the last mouthful of the lolly and read the joke on the stick:

What do you call a gorilla with ear muffs?
Call him what you like, he won't hear you.

The youngster tossed the stick away, his attention now directed once more towards his objective. He walked down the street purposefully, unhooking the plastic radio from his belt again.

'Bodie to Cowley. I'm going in. Over and out,' he said, with a degree of authority.

As he drew closer to the boarded-up shopfront Mark slowed his pace, wondering if he was going to be able to squeeze through the gap by which Prince had gained access. He knelt beside it and peered into the gloom beyond, wrinkling his nose as a particularly noxious stench drifted through the hole.

'Prince,' he called.

The dog usually came running at the sound of his name but Mark waited in vain.

He called again.

Silence greeted his call.

Perhaps the dog had fallen asleep somewhere inside, Mark reasoned. He knew he shouldn't go in, but what the heck, the shop was empty, and he wasn't going to steal anything. He got his head through, then his shoulders, with relative ease. He pulled himself the last few inches, rolling over in the dust which covered the floor. He brushed himself down but his T-shirt and cords were filthy. His mum would go mad when she saw them. He decided he'd better find Prince and return home as quickly as possible.

He straightened up, looking around him at the neglected shelves which formed aisles. It was humid inside the old shop, not as hot as outside but the air smelt stale...

No, it smelt revolting.

He coughed as the nauseating stench enveloped him, growing stronger as he moved cautiously down one aisle towards the rear of the shop. He ran his hand along the shelf as he walked, accidentally disturbing a large beetle. It scuttled away and Mark jumped back in surprise and horror.

'Prince,' he called again, wondering if the dog had perhaps found another way out of the building. He might well have passed straight through the shop and left via a rear exit. If so, Mark thought, he'd have a hard job to find him.

The appalling smell was growing stronger, combining with the cloying warmth to make him feel faint.

He rounded a bank of shelves, preparing to shout the dog's name again.

The sound caught in his throat.

Blood had spread out in a wide puddle, mingling with the dust and slime to form a reeking stain which covered much of the floor in front of Mark. In the centre of the crimson pool lay the twisted remains of the dog, its jaws hanging open, the skull gleaming whitely even in the gloom. Pieces of fur and torn flesh were strewn near the carcass which looked like a blood-soaked rag. One fleshless leg stuck up into the air at an impossible angle.

With morbid curiosity overcoming his initial revulsion, Mark moved towards the remains, almost slipping in the slicks of blood. He reached forward and touched the skull, finding that it was coated by a thick, jelly-like substance which dripped from the rest of the remains like glutinous tears.

Mark felt the stuff on his fingers. He rubbed it between his thumb and forefinger, finally wiping it on his cords.

'Prince,' he said softly, reaching for the dog's collar. He loosened it, pulling the circlet free of the ravaged neck. Blood and sticky fluid coloured his palms as he held the collar before him, eyes still riveted to the bloodied pile of bones and fur which had once been a dog.

He suddenly felt very afraid. He wished he was home with his mum. He'd have to tell her about what happened, perhaps even show her.

Mark turned and ran, scrambling through the gap in the planks, the collar still gripped in one hand. He ran all the way home, holding back his tears.

He wondered why his fingers and hands were beginning to feel so painfully itchy.

Before he reached home, the unpleasant tingling sensation had crept up his arms as far as his elbows. It was as if someone were rubbing his flesh with sandpaper.

Twelve

'Mum, I'm telling you the truth, honest,' Mark Franklin protested. 'I think somebody killed Prince.' The youngster held out the bloodied collar for inspection but his mother didn't touch it.

'You said you saw him squeezing through some planks,' Denise Franklin said. 'He could have cut himself doing it, perhaps pulled his collar off at the same time.'

'There was blood everywhere. He looked like he'd been *eaten*,' Mark insisted.

'Look, Mark, you'd better not say anything about this when your dad gets home, you know how he feels about that sort of thing. He says you watch too much television as it is. You remember those nightmares you had a few months back?'

'I wasn't dreaming what I saw, Mum. I think Prince was eaten by something.'

She shook her head, watching her son over the rim of her teacup. They were both seated at the kitchen table having a bite to eat, but Mark was merely prodding at his food, taking small mouthfuls occasionally, as if he couldn't stomach what lay before him.

'Is there something wrong with that?' Denise asked, nodding in the direction of the plate.

'I'm not very hungry,' he said, wearily, putting down his fork to scratch his other arm. As he did so, Denise noticed how red the skin was. Blotchy in places, it looked as if it had been scalded. Even the palms of his hands were the same. She saw two or three small welts on the flesh of his forearm.

'Are you feeling all right, Mark?' she asked him, wondering if perhaps he'd been out in the sun too long. The temperature that day had hovered around ninety-one degrees and Denise wondered if the boy was suffering from some kind of heat rash. His face, however, looked distinctly pale.

He continued scratching himself.

'Mark,' she repeated. 'I asked if you were feeling all right.'

'I feel a bit sick, Mum,' he told her, finally pushing the plate away. 'I'm going to stay in my room for a while.' He clambered down from the table, swaying uncertainly for a second, then walked out of the room, heading towards his bedroom. Denise drained what was left in her cup, one eye on the dog collar which still lay on the table. She frowned at it, then took a knife and lifted the bloodied circlet and dropped it into the waste-bin, afterwards running the knife beneath the hot tap for a moment to clean it. Then, she put the plates, her own cup and Mark's 'Ghostbusters' mug into the sink and ran some more hot water onto them. That done, Denise strode into the sitting room and pulled a thick book down from the shelves.

'The Encyclopaedia of Family Health,' she read aloud. She flicked through the alphabetical listings, looking for 'Rash', then 'sunburn' (although she doubted if that was really the cause of the reddening on her son's arms). Neither entry offered much help so she flipped through to 'Skin Disorders'. However, there were more than four pages of entries and

Denise couldn't take the time to read the whole lot. She replaced the book and headed down the hall towards Mark's room.

No sounds came from inside and she wondered if he was lying down. Perhaps he'd dropped off to sleep.

She rapped gently on the door.

'Mark! Are you OK, love?' she called.

No answer.

Without waiting to knock again she opened the door and walked in.

Mark was sitting on the edge of the bed staring down at his outstretched arms. He did not lift his head as his mother entered the room.

From elbow to fingertips, on both arms, his skin was a deep crimson, the veins standing out darkly against the swollen flesh. But that wasn't what immediately struck Denise.

It was the liquescent pus-filled boils which caused her to gasp. There were more than half a dozen on each arm, and when he looked up at her, his face a pale mask of fear and pain, she saw that there were also three of the throbbing lesions on his cheeks and forehead.

Denise froze momentarily, not knowing what to do.

Mark didn't move, he merely looked down again at the large swellings which disfigured his arms.

Finally Denise turned and ran back into the sitting room, snatching up the phone. When she got through, the receptionist told her that the doctor was fully booked for the rest of the day and could see no one. Perhaps tomorrow . . .

'My son is very ill,' Denise protested, angrily. 'I have to see the doctor.'

The receptionist asked if she'd like to make an appointment for the following day.

Denise slammed the phone down and stood helplessly for a moment, then snatched up the receiver once more and called for a taxi to pick her and Mark up in ten minutes. Before the despatcher had even confirmed the pick-up, she put the phone down and headed back towards her son's bedroom.

When the time came, she had to practically carry him out to

the waiting cab.

Thirteen

Len Pearson watched the green Fiat pull away from the front door of 25 King Street. He strained his eyes to see if there was any movement inside the house across the street, but without his glasses he could see little. He'd left them on the table beside his armchair, and by the time he retrieved them and returned to his vantage point, the occupant of the house was locking the door and walking away.

She was a good-looking woman in her thirties, large-busted and narrow-waisted, though perhaps a little too broad in the hips.

'Bloody tart,' muttered Len, watching her as she disappeared from view. 'If only your husband knew.'

He was convinced that the woman across the road was having an affair. Every day around lunchtime a green Fiat was parked outside the house for approximately an hour, and then its owner, a man who always wore immaculately-cut suits, emerged from the house and drove away. Len saw these comings and goings, and much more, because he spent most of his time peering out of his sitting room window. But then there wasn't much else he *could* do to pass the time.

At the age of 58, Len Pearson was practically house-bound. He'd worked for British Rail for more than forty years prior to his accident. One winter's day, as he climbed into his engine, his foot had slipped off the cab steps and he'd crashed down between the train and platform. His left leg had been shattered in two places, and after two operations to re-set it, gangrene had set in and the limb had been amputated. Now, with the aid of an artificial leg and a walking frame, he was able to move around his flat with relative ease. But he also had a bad case of chronic bronchitis, and the two infirmities in combination kept him more or less confined to his home.

With that confinement had come bitterness. He had never married and now he lived an isolated existence except for the odd visit from the meals-on-wheels lady and, if he was lucky, the local home-help. She wasn't due again until the end of the week, and all she did anyway was run the hoover around and do a bit of polishing, and the stupid cow always put his ornaments back in the wrong places. Something which greatly annoyed him. Come to think of it, there wasn't much that *didn't* annoy him. He hated the hot weather because it made him sweat. He hated the cold because it played havoc with his arthritis. He disliked the home-help because she was always telling him not to complain, and the meals-on-wheels woman because she simply talked too much.

Len moved away from the window, taking one last look at the house across the street. There was no doubt about it, that bloody woman was up to no good. Little wonder she attracted the men, he thought, flouncing around with no bra, wearing skirts split up to the top of her bloody thigh. She might as well stick a red light over the door. Len grunted. He wouldn't put even *that* past her. For all he knew there might well be other men visitors who called there. He made a mental note to keep his eyes open for any others who might turn up in future.

The young couple in the flat next door to him weren't much better. Bloody newly-weds. They acted as if they'd just discovered sex. Many a night, Len had stood by the wall adjoining their bedroom listening to the laughter and moans coming from within. He was certain they'd break the bed one of these nights. They were away on holiday at the moment so he was getting a bit of peace and quiet until they returned. It was probably one of those 'Club' holidays, or whatever they called them. Len had read about them in the Sunday papers. People only went on them for one thing. If they didn't shag everything that moved then they hadn't had a good time. Getting pissed every night and screwing around at every opportunity. Yes, he knew the type of thing.

The girl on the other side of him was oriental. She was hardly ever home and Len could only guess at what she did for a living. Probably a stripper or something. But he'd noticed that when she *was* home she never had any men in her flat. More than likely a bloody lesbian. Yes, he knew the type.

People nowadays, he thought, didn't seem to have any backbone. The kids were scum, all bloody glue-sniffers or drunks by the time they were twenty. The parents were no better. Marriages breaking up, blokes mucking around with other blokes' wives and the women, like that tart across the road, flaunting themselves for all to see.

Len shook his head in disgust. He knew what went on in this so-called enlightened society and it sickened him. The world was made up of hooligans, slags, con-men and degenerates.

He knew, he read *The News of the World*.

His stomach rumbled and he muttered to himself. He was sure the fish that the meals-on-wheels woman had given him had been off. Complaining about falling standards, he made his way to the bathroom. Balancing delicately on his good leg, supported by his frame, he unfastened his trousers, pulled them down and plonked himself on the toilet.

The slug slithered soundlessly up from the lavatory pan, its eye stalks extending as it broke the surface of the clear water. Half a dozen more followed it, their black shapes resembling animated faeces as they crawled up the white porcelain.

Len shifted position on the plastic seat and murmured something to himself about the meals-on-wheels woman. She'd given him a boiled egg the day before last, silly cow, he was probably constipated now.

More slugs spilled through the pipe, clogging the pan with their numbers, swarming over each other as they dragged their swollen bodies up the gleaming surface.

The closest of them had reached the plastic seat.

He'd tell her next time she called, Len decided. He'd tell the old bag what she'd done to him, how she'd buggered up his insides with her lousy food. He'd . . .

Pain, intense, excruciating pain suddenly tore through him and he cried out. A guttural, rasping groan.

Three of the largest slugs were eating their way into the meaty part of his buttocks while a fourth pushed its obscene form into Len's anus, the lubricating slime helping its passage as it found access to his bowels.

Blood burst from the wounds, spraying the white porcelain and the seething mass of slugs which oozed up the sides of the lavatory in search of food. More of them began digging into the tops of his thighs, and from the waist down he felt as if his body was on fire. Two of the black monstrosities glided up between his legs and Len shrieked with renewed ferocity as they chewed through the soft skin of his scrotum. The fleshy sac seemed to burst and one purple, egg-shaped object dropped into the pan. Blood was now flowing thickly and freely into the lavatory and it further incensed those slugs who had not yet reached the feast.

More and more poured up from the crimson depths seeking the flesh they needed to sustain them.

Len tried to rise but he overbalanced and sprawled helplessly on the floor of the bathroom, his frame clattering over in front of him.

Another slug penetrated his anus, joining its bloated companion in a murderous act of blood-stained sodomy. Fragments of excretion leeked from the riven lower bowel, mingling with the blood which was now spreading across the floor in a sticky pool.

More slugs came swarming over the rim of the lavatory, gliding down the other side, slithering onto Len to feast on his writhing body. He felt one last mind-numbing eruption of pain as the leading slug finally ate its way up into his belly, and then, mercifully, he blacked out.

Some of the creatures tried to chew into his false leg but they soon realized that this was not what they sought and they moved on up his ravaged form until they reached the small of his back, where they plunged their razor-sharp central teeth into the flesh and began feeding. Before long they had bored their way through to his kidneys.

Across the street, the woman from number 25 had returned.

There was another car parked outside the house now, and she smiled as she saw it. The woman glanced up towards the window of Len Pearson's flat, trying to catch a glimpse of the old bastard at the window. She'd seen him spying on her. Well, it didn't bother her. Sod him. Let him carry on looking, and if he didn't like what he saw then tough luck.

But as she entered her front door and glanced back once again at Len's window, she saw no sign of his hunched figure skulking behind the curtains.

Perhaps he'd found something better to occupy his time, she thought.

Fourteen

Finch glanced at his watch as he dried his hands. It was almost three in the afternoon. His last patient had been dealt with, and he now had two hours until the evening surgery. He decided to nip out for something to eat. He'd had nothing since breakfast. His two partners had already finished and departed. Finch closed his briefcase and was about to leave the room when he heard a commotion from outside.

Raised voices.

One of them he recognized as June, the receptionist.

'Surgery is not open again until five . . .'

'I have to see him *now*. My son can't be left like this all afternoon!'

'I'll ask the doctor . . .'

'You *must* let me in!'

Finch opened the door and looked out to see June barring it, as if protecting him from another, slightly older woman

81

who was holding a young lad close to her.

'What's going on, June?' Finch asked.

'I must see you, doctor. It's my little boy,' Denise Franklin blurted.

'This lady has no appointment and...'

Finch took one look at the boy and barely managed to conceal his surprise.

Mark Franklin's face was almost completely covered in bulbous, festering sores.

'Come in,' Finch said, looking straight past his receptionist. He ushered Denise and Mark into his room, then turned to June. 'It's all right, June, I can manage.'

He stepped back into the room and closed the door behind him. Mark was sitting on one of the two leather-bound seats facing the doctor's desk and Finch crossed to him immediately, noting a glazed look in the boy's eyes as well as the all-too-obvious infection of the skin.

'What's his name?' Finch asked, without taking his eyes off the boy.

Denise told him.

'What's wrong with him, doctor?' she added.

Finch ignored the question. 'Is his condition recent?' he asked. 'Did it begin without warning? I mean, these lesions.'

'When he went out this morning he was fine,' Denise said.

'He's been in contact with nothing corrosive?'

'What's that?'

'Acid, strong solvent, anything like that?'

'No. Not that I know of.'

Finch placed a thermometer in the boy's mouth, then removed a wooden spatula from its sterilized plastic wrapping and prodded the edges of one of the sores as cautiously as he could.

The skin stretched and looked as if it was going to break. Mark whimpered softly, keeping the thermometer in his mouth.

Finch waited a moment longer, then removed the thin glass tube. The mercury was nudging 101. If the boy was suffering from the same illness as Molly Foster then it was in a far more advanced state, Finch thought. He asked Mark to remove his T-shirt which, with difficulty, he did.

His back and chest were also dotted with the suppurating sores.

'We'll need to get him to a hospital,' Finch said. 'I can't deal with this here.'

'But what is it?' Denise Franklin demanded.

He wondered whether he should mention Molly Foster and the frightening similarity of her disfigurement, but he decided to remain silent.

'Can't you give him anything?' Denise pleaded.

'Only pain killers if he needs them, Mrs Franklin. I'm dealing with something which even *I* don't understand. I've never encountered anything quite like this before.' He turned to Mark. 'Are you in pain, Mark?'

The boy looked at his mother as if waiting to be given the answer. Then he glanced at Finch and nodded almost imperceptibly. The doctor reached for his prescription pad.

'I don't want to go to hospital,' Mark said, swallowing with some difficulty. 'Please don't make me go.'

'If you don't go, Mark, you'll become even more ill,' Finch said. 'You don't want that, do you?'

'I don't want to go,' the boy said, tears welling in his eyes.

'What will happen to him if he stays at home?' Denise asked.

'If he does then *I* can't take any responsibility for his well-being,' Finch told her, bluntly.

'I want him with me,' Denise said.

Finch bit his lip and fixed the woman in an icy stare.

'You realize the risk you're taking?' he said. 'If it turns out to be a contagious disease of some kind then you and your husband are also at risk.'

'Please don't make me go to hospital,' Mark pleaded again, that glazed look returning to his eyes. Finch felt as if he were staring into two opaque marbles when he looked at the boy.

'All right,' he said finally, 'but take this.' He scribbled something on a piece of paper. 'It's my home phone number. If there's any deterioration in his condition let me know. It

83

doesn't matter what time of the night it is.' He passed her the paper. 'I'll call in tomorrow and check on him.'

'I think he'll feel happier at home, doctor,' said Denise, getting to her feet.

'If he hasn't improved by tomorrow, Mrs Franklin, then you'd be foolish not to let him undergo hospital tests.'

'I don't trust hospitals,' she said sharply.

Finch didn't answer.

'May I have your address, please?' he said, wearily.

'Number five St Anne's Court,' Denise replied.

Finch frowned and slowed the speed of his writing for a moment. St Anne's Court. He knew that name from somewhere.

'We'd better go, doctor,' she told him. 'There's a taxi waiting outside for us.' She promised to ring if necessary.

Finch waited until he heard the footsteps recede down the corridor, then he sat back in his chair, staring at what he'd written, thinking about what he'd just seen. Could it be a contagious disease of some kind, he wondered? Then again, he knew of no disease which manifested symptoms as severe as those he'd seen on the boy and on Molly Foster. Besides, if it was that vehement, why hadn't Lisa been infected? Why not the boy's parents? Finch tapped his pen on top of his desk, glancing once more at the address before him. His eyes suddenly widened and he got to his feet, crossing the room to a map of central London which was pinned to the notice board on the far wall. He ran his finger over it until he found the area he sought.

'St Anne's Court,' he whispered.

Now he knew why the name rang a bell.

Mark Franklin lived just one street away from Molly Foster.

Finch massaged the bridge of his nose between thumb and forefinger, his forehead wrinkling into a frown.

With both victims living so close together, could it be coincidence?

He hoped, for reasons he was not yet sure of, that it was.

Fifteen

The boy lay in the darkness listening to the ticking of the clock.

Unable to sleep because of the steadily growing pain, he shifted from his back to his side, then onto his stomach but the position change only aggravated his discomfort, so finally Mark Franklin swung himself out of bed and flicked on his bedside light. He opened his pyjama jacket, gazing down at his body with eyes like glass.

The whole of his chest and abdomen was a festering mass of oozing sores. He could feel them on his back too, the swollen tips brushing against the light material of his pyjamas. But despite the pain he did not cry out, he merely got slowly to his feet and headed for the door of his room.

His mother had told him that, if he felt bad, he should call out and either she or his father would come to him. They would call the doctor if things got too unbearable.

Moving somewhat unsteadily on legs which by this time were also ulcerated, he padded down the hall to the bathroom and tugged at the long, dangling cord. The light flickered into life and Mark moved to the sink where he gazed at his reflection in the large mirror. One eye was nearly closed due to the discoloured sore which was forming on the lid, the other was bloodshot and glazed. He gripped the sides of the sink for a moment as the pain jabbed red hot knives into him. His head was throbbing madly, as if someone had set a steam-hammer going inside it. Waves of nausea swept through him but he retained his balance, reaching for the door of the medicine cabinet.

He took down his father's safety razor and slowly, painfully, unscrewed the blade, releasing it. The wickedly sharp edge glinted as Mark inspected it, hardly able to feel the thin sliver of steel between his bloated fingers.

After a moment or two he crossed to the door again, pulled the light cord and walked slowly down the hall.

The door to his parents room was open, as were the windows. The curtains, stirred by the light warm breeze, waved gently and Mark stood in the doorway watching them for a moment, as if hypnotized by the softly flowing material. However, his attention finally turned to the sleeping forms of his parents.

Both Roger and Denise Franklin were naked, only a sheet covering them. As Mark moved closer he saw the soft rise and fall of his father's broad chest, the single bead of perspiration glistening on his forehead.

He lifted the razor blade in swollen fingers, his entire body feeling as if it were on fire. The light from the hall glinted on the blade's vicious edge.

Mark steadied the blade in his hand, then swiftly drew it twice across his father's throat.

The sheer steel sliced effortlessly through skin and muscle, opening veins and arteries which immediately began spurting forth fountains of blood, some of which splattered Mark. But he stood by unperturbed as the two cuts seemed to widen and finally join, forming one massive rent. The edges quivered like lips around a blood-filled mouth. Crimson sprayed wildly from the deep slash, the blood from the severed carotid arteries rising a full three feet, propelled by the pumping of the heart. The crimson cascade hit the wall behind the bed and ran down like paint thrown at a canvas.

Roger Franklin's eyes jerked open, the whites standing out in stark contrast to the pupils as the orbs bulged in their sockets. The pain from the wound was minimal but he could feel the powerful jets of crimson bursting from his body with a force that caused him to convulse. He opened his mouth to scream but he could not. The bitter taste of his own life fluid filled his mouth before it ran down from both corners, bubbling over his lips to form a thick purple foam as it mixed with the saliva.

Mark moved away from his dying father, the razor blade still held in his fingers.

He walked quickly but unhurriedly around to the other side of the bed where his mother was now awake, hurtled into consciousness by the cascade of blood beside her. She saw her husband's body jerking wildly as he clawed at the huge gash in his neck, the blood jetting through his fingers. The walls, the bed, her own body were all covered in the warm red fluid. There were even spots of it on the ceiling. She shook her head in disbelief and horror as he turned towards her, his eyes rolling upwards in the sockets to reveal the whites. He made a liquid gurgling sound and then lay still, his hands falling to his sides. A soft rumbling, followed by a pungent smell, signalled that his sphincter muscle had relaxed.

Denise was barely aware of Mark standing beside her.

He brought the razor blade down in a swatting action and she screamed as the steel gashed her arm from shoulder to elbow. She tried to roll off the bed but her escape route was blocked by the body of her husband.

Mark struck again, slicing open the sole of one flailing foot, then, with another lightning blow, her calf.

Still screaming, she practically threw herself across Roger's body, landing with a thud on the carpet, the wind momentarily knocked from her. As she tried to stand a searing pain shot up her cut leg and she toppled over once more, blood soaking into the carpet as it pumped from the hideous gashes.

Mark followed, moving purposefully around the bed, his blank eyes fixing her in an emotionless stare. He watched her claw her way up onto her knees, tears now streaming down her cheeks as she saw him advancing on her. She called his name, a note of pleading in her voice along with sheer, uncomprehending terror.

He struck again, catching her across the right breast, puncturing the soft flesh, almost severing the nipple.

She screamed again and reached for something to ward him

off, her hand closing around the bedside lamp. As she reached for it he raked the razor blade down her back, feeling it scrape on bone as it carved across her right shoulder blade. Blood ran down her back but she turned and brought the lamp crashing down on his head, the impact knocking him backwards. He crashed to the floor, the razor blade slipping from his fingers.

As he hit the carpet he screamed in agony. The boils on his back burst in unison, gouts of evil-smelling pus pumping from the torn lesions.

Through tears of pain and desperation, Denise saw her son writhing before her as more and more of the running sores began to burst. Thick yellow fluid exploded from them until it seemed that his entire upper body was a liquescent mass. It was as if his entire torso and face had been transformed into one giant festering pustule. His skin seemed to peel away and now blood was mingling with the sticky discharge which oozed from the burst boils.

Mark shrieked, his limbs going rigid as new waves of pain tore through him, and Denise could only watch helplessly, the life draining rapidly from her own body. Her vision was dimming as she slipped towards unconsciousness, but she could still see the motionless form of her husband lying on the bed, some of his spilled blood beginning to congeal thickly, while beside her on the floor her son was undergoing the last involuntary spasms which signalled the end of his life.

The room smelt like a charnel house, the pungent odours of blood, pus and excrement mingling together to form one stomach-turning stench of death.

Denise Franklin felt the blood draining from her. She felt searing pain from the four wounds. With a last despairing moan she collapsed.

The banging on the front door began less than thirty seconds later.

Sixteen

At first he thought he was dreaming. That the strident ringing of the phone was inside his head. But as he forced his eyes open he realized it wasn't his imagination.

The ringing continued.

As Finch reached for the receiver he mumbled something about late nights. It seemed barely two or three hours since he'd climbed beneath the sheets. Now his regular alarm call was signalling the start of another day.

He blinked hard and checked his watch.

3.00 a.m.

He picked up the receiver, stifling a yawn.

'Hello,' he croaked, wondering why anyone should be calling at this ungodly hour of the morning.

The voice at the other end sounded sharp and alert and Finch shook himself, feeling at something of a disadvantage.

'Dr Alan Finch?' the voice asked.

'Yes. Who is this?' He could not prevent himself yawning this time.

'My name is Nicholson. Detective Sergeant Nicholson. Could you come to number five St Anne's Court? Now, please. We can send a car for you...'

Nicholson allowed the sentence to trail off.

Finch rubbed his eyes, still somewhat bemused.

'No, it's OK,' he said. 'I'll drive.' There was a moment's silence, finally broken by the doctor. 'What's happened?' he asked.

'You'll see when you get here,' he was told, then Nicholson hung up, leaving Finch to stare at the buzzing receiver. He replaced it slowly onto the cradle, stretched once, listening to his joints pop and crack, then he got to his feet and began dressing.

Within ten minutes he was behind the wheel of his Chevette, heading towards his appointed destination.

The streets were understandably deserted and he drove with ease, glimpsing just one other vehicle. The journey would normally have taken him close to forty-five minutes but he made it in under thirty. As he pulled the car into a parking space opposite the flats in St. Anne's Court, he saw two police cars and an ambulance parked in the road and on the pavement outside the building. The blue lights of the ambulance were turning silently, and as he climbed out of the car, it seemed to Finch as if he had entered a strange soundless world. He almost longed for the screech of sirens to break the oppressive silence. Lights were burning in some of the windows and he caught sight of a figure peering out at him as he approached the flats.

A uniformed policeman standing at the door asked him who he was. Finch took out an identity card and passed it to the policeman, who checked the unflattering photo against its owner's features for a second before returning it. Finch proceeded up the stairs.

He found more policemen outside the flat and had to repeat the identification procedure before being allowed inside.

There were at least half a dozen plain-clothes men moving about in the sitting room and hallway of the flat, occasionally disappearing into a room at the far end of the long hall. Then a man with long hair and a corduroy jacket emerged from the room. He looked at Finch and attempted a smile but decided against it, choosing instead to shake hands with the doctor.

'Doctor Finch?' he said. 'I'm Detective Sergeant Nicholson. Come this way, please.'

As he entered the room, Finch almost recoiled from the vile smell which hung in the air. He saw three other men in the room, one of whom was taking photographs of the carnage. Of the blood-drenched walls and bed and of the three bodies which lay sprawled like disfigured mannequins.

Finch had seen dead bodies many times before, road accident casualties and victims of muggings or industrial accidents, but nothing he had seen could compare with the horror of the sight which he now looked upon.

As he stared at the corpse of young Mark Franklin, the skin mottled red and blue, raw and bleeding, Finch suddenly felt a stab of guilt. Was it guilt? He lowered his head slightly. If only he had insisted that the boy be admitted to hospital instead of allowing the mother to talk him out of it. Perhaps the boy, at least, would not now be dead.

He glanced at the other two bodies and shook his head slowly. One of the men who had been in the room when he entered now approached him and introduced himself.

'Sorry to get you out of bed, Doctor Finch,' Detective Inspector Grogan added, lighting up a cigarette. 'Especially for this little lot.' He gestured towards the bodies.

'Why did you call *me*?' Finch wanted to know.

'You were the boy's doctor, weren't you?' the DI said.

Finch nodded.

'We found your phone number on a pad in the living room.' The policeman blew out a stream of smoke. 'What was wrong with the boy?'

Finch sighed.

'I wish I knew,' he faltered, then corrected himself. 'I wish I'd *known*.'

'How long had you been treating him?' Grogan wanted to know.

Finch told him about the visit that afternoon, about wanting to have the boy admitted to hospital. Grogan listened without taking his eyes from the doctor, merely nodding occasionally.

'Why is the boy's illness so much of a concern to you?' Finch asked finally.

'Because he murdered his parents,' said the DI in a matter-of-fact tone. He held out his hand and Nicholson handed him a plastic envelope.

It contained the bloodied razor blade.

'He used this,' Grogan continued.

Finch ran a hand through his hair, looking first at the razor blade then at the bodies.

'A neighbour heard screams. She gave us a call. All three of them were dead when we arrived. The father had been dead about twenty minutes, the mother had bled to death and the boy . . . we're not sure about.' There was a momentary silence while the policeman took another long drag on his cigarette. 'You were his doctor but you say you don't know what was wrong with him.'

'May I look at the body?' Finch asked and Grogan stepped aside.

Kneeling beside the corpse was George Bennett. He was taking skin samples with a small scalpel, dropping them into a series of thin glass test tubes which he then sealed and placed carefully in his pocket. The pathologist smiled thinly at Finch as he joined him. The doctor could clearly see the deep welts and craters in the skin where the boils had burst. Some of the pus had formed a sticky film on the skin, but in other places it had hardened into a scab-like coating.

'Have you ever seen anything like it before?' Bennett asked him.

Finch shuddered involuntarily as he thought of Molly Foster.

Was the same thing happening to her now? He wondered whether or not he should mention the other woman. He decided not to.

For the moment, anyway.

'When are the autopsies being carried out?' he asked.

'As soon as the bodies are taken back to Scotland Yard,' Bennett told him.

'Why do you want to know?' Grogan inquired.

'Well, the lad *was* my patient,' Finch said. 'I'd like to be there when it's done.'

'That's not the way we do things, I'm afraid, doctor. But you will be told as soon as we have anything worth telling you.'

'Is there some objection to me being present?' Finch asked.

Grogan looked at Bennett.

'It doesn't matter to me,' the pathologist said. 'And I'm sure it won't matter to those poor sods.' He hooked a thumb in the direction of the trio of corpses.

'What are you hoping to see, doctor?' the DI asked.

'I wish I knew,' Finch told him. 'Perhaps it'll help me find some answers.'

'Just lately,' Grogan sighed, 'answers seem to be in short supply.'

All three men turned once more to gaze at the dead bodies which littered the room.

Seventeen

The summer night was a warm and humid one, but in the pathology lab it was like autumn. The temperature was kept down to a steady fifty-eight degrees, although neither Finch nor Bennett noticed the chill in the air. The pathologist was washing his hands at a sink on one side of the room, while Finch sat close to the stainless steel slab which bore the body of Mark Franklin. He was looking down at the boy, almost mesmerized by the appalling appearance of the corpse. It looked as if someone had blasted the youngster with a flame-thrower. And if they had, Finch mused, his remains couldn't have smelt much worse than they did now.

On the other two slabs behind him lay the bodies of Denise and Roger Franklin, both covered by white plastic sheets, only the feet protruding from beneath the thin coverlets. Attached to the right big toe of each corpse was a tag bearing the name, weight, height and time of admittance.

Finch looked across to the trolley which stood beside the first slab. There was a thick rubber sheet laid on it, and spread out on that was an assortment of scalpels, saws and long bladed knives. He also saw what looked like a large pair of bolt-cutters, the implement he knew would be employed to open up the ribcage when the time came. There was also an appliance very much like a dentist's drill, except that it bore a small metal wheel, serrated around its edge. On the end of the trolley there was something which Finch did not expect to see.

A carton of yoghurt.

'My breakfast,' said Bennett apologetically, removing the carton from the trolley. 'At least it keeps cool down here.' His smile faded slowly and he looked at the body of Mark Franklin. 'You know, there's an old saying,' he began wearily. '"The psychiatrist knows all and does nothing. The surgeon knows nothing and does all. The dermatologist knows nothing and does nothing."' He paused. '"The pathologist knows everything, but a day too late."'

'Very philosophical,' said Finch, attempting a smile which didn't quite materialize.

Bennett raised his eyebrows matter-of-factly, then reached up and activated the tape-recorder. He pulled the microphone closer to him.

'The victim has been weighed, all items of clothing have been itemized and prepared for analysis. External examination follows. I shall omit anal smears and nail scrapings as these are not felt to be necessary. If requested they will be carried out. The same applies to any other rudimentary external tests.' He paused for a moment, picking up a small scalpel which he used to raise a flap of skin which had once formed the sheath of a reeking pustule. 'The entire body is covered by lesions the origin of which is not yet known.' Reaching back onto the trolley he picked up a syringe, ran it into one of the large pustules and drew off as much of the thick liquid as he could. He deposited it in a Petri dish which he then sealed.

Returning to the body, Bennett took another syringe and drew 25ml of blood from the boy's arm. Still nattering to the tape recorder as Finch looked on silently, the pathologist

94

announced that he was going to begin the internal examination.

He took a large, long-bladed scalpel and made a Y-shaped incision which ran from throat to pubic region, curving slightly to avoid the navel. That done, he pulled the torso open with his hands as if he were unwrapping a present, folding back the flaps of skin to expose the glistening tangle of viscera within. An almost palpable blast of foul-smelling air rose from the cavity and both men wrinkled their noses. The pathologist prodded and poked the various organs curiously.

'There doesn't appear to be any damage to internal organs,' he said into the tape recorder. 'I will remove the thorax section now.'

Bennett picked up the large bolt-cutter-like instrument and cut quickly and efficiently through the ribcage. The sound of snapping bone filled the room and Finch watched as the lungs and oesophagus were exposed. The heart too, now still and greyish in colour, was visible amongst the other organs. All were slightly shrunken. The pathologist removed the lungs and the remainder of the section and carefully laid it in a large stainless steel dish. A dribble of dark fluid came from the lungs, followed by several large, almost black clots of blood.

He followed the same procedure with the stomach and intestines, holding the entrails as if they were bulging, slippery lengths of bloated spaghetti. These he placed in a separate dish for weighing and then more detailed scrutiny. The entire chest and abdominal cavity was now empty.

Wiping one hand on his apron, the pathologist switched off the tape recorder.

'I think we'll have a look at those samples before we open the skull,' he said. Picking up the Petri dish and the syringe full of blood, he carried them to one of the laboratory workbenches, followed by Finch. Using the end of a scalpel, Bennett took some of the pus from the dish and smeared it on a microscope slide. He repeated the procedure with a droplet of the blood, then slid the first slide beneath the powerful lens, adjusting a knob until the image swam into focus.

Finch saw him frown.

'Have a look at that,' he said, stepping back.

The doctor pressed close to the eyepiece and squinted through it at the slide. It was matter taken from one of the sores.

Thousands of tiny snake-like shapes writhed beneath his gaze.

'Pus is basically a combination of white blood cells and dead bacteria,' said Finch. 'If anything, these cells should be spherical.'

'Have a look at the blood sample,' Bennett suggested, pushing the slide towards him. Finch slid the second slide beneath the lens and adjusted the magnification.

The same snake-like entities were present.

'These bacteria should be dead,' he commented, a note of puzzlement in his voice. He continued gazing at the millions of writhing shapes before him, invisible but for the incredible enlarging powers of the microscope.

Bennett had already got to his feet and returned to the body of Mark Franklin, switching on the tape recorder again.

'I'm going to open the skull,' he said into the microphone. With that he picked up the slim object which resembled the dentist's drill, checked that it was plugged in and switched it on. The circular blade on the end spun with a high pitched whine and the pathologist seemed satisfied. He switched it off, took a scalpel and carefully cut a line through the skin of the boy's forehead, just below the hairline. Then, as Finch rejoined him, he activated the electric saw once again, lowering the spinning blade until it made contact with bone. There was a sound like fingernails on a blackboard as the skull was cut open.

Finch watched Bennett put down the cutting instrument and slowly pry the skull lid up, using the scalpel as a lever, revealing an inch or two of brain. Finally he pulled the encasing bone free as if he were removing a hat, exposing the greyish-pink meat inside the head. Using another scalpel, he cut a thin segment away and laid it on a third microscope slide.

The pathologist then studied his sample beneath the powerful lens. He sighed and stepped back, motioning Finch forward.

'What do you make of it?' Bennett asked.

Looking through the microscope, the doctor shook his head almost imperceptibly.

Even the portion of brain contained the black, writhing shapes.

They appeared to have no discernible features save for their reptilian shape. At first they reminded Finch a little of sperm cells, but he could see no head. There was just that writhing, whip-lash shape, tapering slightly at either end.

'Could it be a virus?' he wondered aloud.

'You're the doctor. What do you think?' Bennett asked him. 'Personally, I don't think it is,' he added.

'Well, I'll admit I've never seen cells like that before in a viral infection.' The doctor stroked his chin thoughtfully and looked at the pathologist. 'What do *you* think it is?'

'Those black shapes don't look like bacteria,' Bennett said. 'And also, the chances are that most of them would have died out by now if they had been. I think they're blood flukes of some kind.'

Finch looked back at the brain section, studying the wriggling shapes.

'Well,' he said, quietly. 'If they are, they're certainly not of human origin.'

Friday – the 14th

Eighteen

Dawn was hauling itself sluggishly across the sky as Finch brought the Chevette to a halt outside number five Flaxman Court. He had driven fast from Scotland Yard, perhaps a little too fast. On one occasion, in the Haymarket, he'd run a red light, but fortunately traffic was light and no one had been in his way. Now he almost sprinted from the car towards the steps which would take him up to the flat. His mind was in a turmoil over what he had seen both in the flat at St Anne's Court, around the corner, and at the police laboratory. If Mark Franklin, by some chance, had been suffering from the same disease as Molly Foster, then there was every reason to suspect that *she* would suffer the same fate. He felt it his duty to tell Lisa Foster, no matter how shocked she might be. There seemed every possibility that Molly was in grave danger, and if that was the case, Lisa had a right to know. As he climbed the steps he wondered how he was going to break it to her.

The door of the flat suddenly opened and Lisa stepped out.

Both of them froze for a moment, gazing at one another, shivering in the early-morning breeze. It was Lisa who broke the silence.

'Alan, what are you doing here?' she wanted to know.

He noticed, even in the subdued half-light, that her face looked pale and drawn. There were dark rings beneath her eyes, as if someone had smudged her lower lids with charcoal. She wore a voluminous black coat which hid her shapely figure, flapping around her like a cape when she walked.

Finch was struggling to decide if he should tell her the real

101

reason for his presence when they heard a car pull up across the street. Finch saw that it was a taxi, and the driver was peering across at the flats.

'I've got to go,' Lisa said. 'The hospital called. It's my mother.'

Finch clenched his teeth, sucking in an almost painful breath.

'Her condition's deteriorated.' Lisa tried to sidestep him. 'I've got to get to the hospital, Alan,' she insisted.

'I'll take you,' he said, taking her arm, almost pulling her towards his waiting car.

'But the taxi . . .' she protested.

'To hell with the taxi,' Finch snapped and slid behind the steering wheel of the Chevette. He twisted the key in the ignition and the engine roared into life.

The cab driver clambered out of his vehicle as the other car drove off, taking with it his prospective passenger. He watched until it disappeared, swearing to himself, then he got back in and drove off.

'When did the hospital get in touch?' Finch asked, not taking his eyes from the road.

'About ten minutes before you arrived,' Lisa told him. 'They told me I should get over there as quickly as possible.' She studied his profile for a moment. 'Alan, you remember me asking you if you thought she was going to die?'

He nodded.

'She is, isn't she? Otherwise they wouldn't have called me.'

Finch gripped the wheel tighter, trying to disguise the concern in his voice when he spoke.

'Your mother is in the best possible hands,' he said, none too convincingly. 'Did they tell you anything at all about her condition?'

'Only that it had deteriorated and that I should get to the hospital as soon as possible,' she informed him. There was a protracted silence during which her eyes never left him. 'You know something about what's going on, don't you?'

Finch didn't answer. He swung the car around a corner and

the hospital loomed before them.

'I have a right to know,' she persisted. 'Why were you calling at the flat at this time in the morning?'

He sucked in a deep breath.

'A boy died tonight,' he said. 'He murdered his parents first and then he died. He had the same symptoms as your mother.'

'Oh my God,' murmured Lisa, and she was out of the car almost before it had stopped moving, bolting for the main entrance of the hospital, followed closely by Finch. They both dashed into the reception area, past a bewildered night porter who shouted something after them. But they did not hear, and even if they had, they wouldn't have stopped running.

Finch caught up as Lisa reached the lift. As he spun her round he could already see the tears welling in her eyes.

'Lisa, if only I'd known what was wrong with her,' he said. 'But no one knew, they still don't . . .'

The sentence trailed off as the lift arrived, the doors sliding open to allow them access. Both stepped in and leant against the sides of the car as it rose, finally disgorging them on the fifth floor. Lisa ran from the lift, hearing shouts and screams coming from the direction of the ward. Finch ran after her and together they hurtled into the ward.

Lisa looked frantically to her right and left, trying to trace the source of the commotion. As she moved up the corridor she caught sight of Doctor Benton emerging from a side room. His face was covered in perspiration and he looked as if he'd just run ten miles, but when he saw Lisa moving towards him he seemed to recover his composure and attempted to intercept her.

Finch followed.

'Where's my mother?' she blurted, trying to push her way past Benton. 'I got a call saying she was worse and I should come as soon as I could.'

'Yes, I know, but we've had to transfer her to another room,' Benton said.

'I have to see her.'

'That's not a good idea at the moment, Miss Foster,' he told her.

A scream of pain and rage came from the room and the sound caused an icy tingle down Finch's spine.

'There's a nurse in there with her at the moment. We're going to sedate her,' Benton informed them.

'I must see her,' Lisa persisted, trying to manoeuvre herself around Benton, but he continued to bar her way.

There was another scream and Benton looked at Finch.

'Keep her here,' he said, indicating Lisa, then he retreated back into the side room, closing the door behind him. The cries and moans were momentarily muffled.

'Alan, please let me go,' she begged, attempting to pull away from him.

Finch shook his head, his own curiosity now roused, mixed with a terrible foreboding.

'Wait until she's sedated,' he said, his mind straying to the sight of that bedroom where he'd seen the bodies of Mark Franklin and his parents. Could Molly Foster be afflicted in the same way? The shouting, Finch assumed, was coming from Molly and he marvelled at how a woman who was supposedly so ill could muster such shattering roars of pain and anger.

Was it anger?

'You must let me see her,' Lisa pleaded, tears welling up once more in her wide eyes. 'Please, Alan.'

He loosened his grip slightly, and in that split second she managed to escape him, her hands reaching for the door of the room.

He tried to stop her but, together, they blundered inside.

Lisa froze, her eyes riveted to the tableau which met her, to the . . . creature on the bed for, had she not known, she would never have guessed that it was her mother.

Every inch of Molly Foster's skin was swollen and bulging with thick, oozing sores which were continually bursting, weeping their viscous contents onto the sheets. Her eyes were almost closed because of the pustules which had formed around them, and as she tried to lift her arms, the bulk of the swollen flesh made the task look impossible. As the young nurse who was holding the hypodermic needle attempted to grip Molly's arm, she found that she was holding only the sticky discharge of half a dozen boils which burst as they were touched. It was as if someone had pumped the woman's body up with compressed air, filling it to bursting point with the thick yellow mess which was pumping from so many of the throbbing lesions.

'Get her out of here,' Benton yelled at Finch.

In that split second, Molly managed to pull loose from the nurse's grip. The hypodermic flew into the air as the nurse was knocked to the ground by a ferocious back-hand swipe. She crashed into a trolley, knocking it over, yelping in pain as scalpels and knives fell onto her, cutting her in half a dozen places.

Molly swung herself out of bed, her yellowed eyes fixed on Lisa.

Benton made a grab for the discarded hypodermic but Molly's bloated fingers closed around it first and she lashed out at the doctor, who just managed to avoid the thrust. The nurse, by this time, had struggled to her feet and she came at Molly from behind, trying to wrest the sharp hypo from her swollen hand. Molly spun round and thrust again.

The needle buried itself in the nurse's eye, snapping off half-way as she fell, blood running down her cheek like crimson tears. She screamed in agony and tried to pluck out the thin probe but her blood and spurting vitreous fluid made it impossible. She rolled onto her side and lay still.

With the remainder of the needle glinting evilly beneath the fluorescents, Molly moved towards her daughter, holding the syringe up like a knife.

Lisa could only shake her head in horrified disbelief until she felt strong arms pulling her away from the monstrous creature which had once been her mother, but now looked like something that had stepped straight from a nightmare. Molly opened her mouth as if to say something but all that came forth was a low wail of agony and she stopped in her tracks, her body jerking as if electricity were being pumped through it. She dropped the needle and clapped both hands to her face as the boils began to erupt, spewing thick yellow fluid everywhere. Her whole body was quivering madly now and she dropped to her knees, the pustules on her legs bursting with a series of obscene splattering sounds as she crushed them.

Finch tried to turn Lisa's head away but he too found himself mesmerized by the appalling sight before him. Benton had dashed out into the corridor to find help.

The nurse, her eye pierced by the snapped needle, still lay motionless.

Molly Foster raised a defiant hand towards her daughter and then, with an agonized moan, she fell forward and did not move again.

Finch moved away from Lisa and rushed to Molly's side. He turned her over carefully, anxious not to allow any of the thick yellow fluid to get on his hands, and looked closely at her face which was now cratered by dozens of deep holes, some of them spilling a thin stream of blood onto the floor. It appeared that almost all of the boils had burst, even those around her eyes, and the hardening pus had almost welded the lids together. The stench which rose from the body was frightful.

Lisa clutched her stomach, gagged and turned away, fighting back the urge to vomit, but as she caught a glimpse of the dead nurse she finally lost the struggle and retched violently.

Staggering out into the corridor, she saw Benton returning, accompanied by two interns and a nurse. The nurse stayed with Lisa until some of the colour came back into her cheeks, then she followed her companions into the room.

No one spoke for long moments until Benton finally broke the silence.

'Get the bodies out of here,' he said, wearily. 'Down to pathology immediately.'

One of the interns hurried off to fetch a gurney.

Finch pulled a blanket from the bed and covered both Molly and the dead nurse.

'I didn't expect anything like this to happen,' said Benton, quietly.

Finch seemed to ignore the comment.

'When will the autopsy be performed on Mrs Foster?' he asked.

'Not until the pathologist arrives in the morning. Why?'

Finch looked out into the corridor at Lisa, who was leaning against the far wall with her head bowed, crying softly.

'Get somebody to take care of her until I've finished,' he said, softly.

'Finished what?' Benton wanted to know.

'I want to look at Mrs Foster's body before the pathologist comes in. There's something I've got to find out.'

Finch looked on silently as the corpse of Molly Foster was pushed into the selected cold drawer. The array of doors reminded him of a large filing cabinet. There were enough compartments to hold fifteen bodies, but only those of Molly Foster and the dead nurse were stored there at the moment. They would rest in the coffin-sized compartments until the pathologist arrived.

Finch looked at the syringe in his hand, at the 25 ml of blood which he'd drawn from the body of Molly Foster only moments earlier. Then he went to the microscope which stood on a work-bench nearby and selected a slide, forcing a droplet of the blood from the syringe onto the thin glass section. He sandwiched it with another, then slipped it beneath the probing lens of the microscope.

The slide was alive with moving shapes and Finch swallowed hard.

The snake-like organisms which writhed furiously beneath his gaze were identical to those he'd seen earlier at the police lab.

Nineteen

As he drove, Finch looked across at Lisa who was gazing blankly out of the window, her hands knitted together in her lap. Her cheeks were tear-stained, her eyes red-rimmed. He wondered if she was going to start crying again. They had left the hospital ten minutes earlier, but only in the last few moments had she stopped sobbing. Finch had tried to persuade her to stay in hospital for a day or two or at least seek the comfort of a tranquilizer, but she had declined both suggestions. She sniffed and pulled a tissue from her handbag.

'I'm sorry,' she said, her words almost inaudible.

'I'm the one who should be sorry,' he said with genuine remorse. 'If I could have done something for your mother in the first place . . .' He allowed the words to trail off.

'You did everything you could,' she told him, her gaze still fixed outside the car. She felt a shiver run through her, and for a moment she thought the tears were going to flood once again, but she clenched her fists and managed to fight them back. There was another protracted silence, then Lisa spoke again. 'Why did she kill that nurse?'

Finch opened his mouth to speak but she did not give him time.

'Alan, she was trying to kill me too.'

She finally looked across at him and he saw a single tear trickle down her cheek. Lisa brushed it away with the tissue.

Finch felt angry with himself. Angry because he had been unable to help either Molly Foster or Mark Franklin but also because he felt so helpless. The disease (if that was the correct word) which had claimed their lives was completely unknown to him and he felt at a disadvantage. Mixed with his anger, though, was fear. If it was a disease of some kind then the two who had died so far might not be the only sufferers. He pondered on how many people were, at this moment, undergoing agonies similar to those suffered by his other two patients. It was too much to hope that they were isolated cases, wasn't it?

He brought the car to a halt outside the flats and Lisa reached for the door handle. As she did, he noticed that she was shaking. He leant across to open the door for her.

'Thank you for your help tonight,' she said to him, still clutching the balled-up tissue.

'If there's anything at all that I can do, promise you'll ring me,' Finch said.

She tried to smile but it wouldn't come.

'I promise,' she told him and pushed herself out of the car.

The doctor watched as she made her way across the road to the flats, climbing the stairs wearily until she reached the door of number five. He saw her disappear inside. Only then did he put the car in gear and pull away.

Lisa Foster stood in the gloom of the sitting room for a moment, her back pressed to the door. She closed her eyes and sucked in a deep breath, pausing briefly before she went through to the kitchen. As she filled the kettle she noticed that her hands were still shaking. Spooning sugar into her cup she spilled some on the table, but it didn't seem to bother her. She sat down and waited for the kettle to boil, running her index finger around the rim of the cup. If there was anything to be thankful for in this entire tragedy, it was that she would not be called to identify her mother's body. Lisa knew that she could not have tolerated standing over the ravaged corpse again. A vision of her dead mother swam briefly into her mind and she brushed away the tears once more, surprised that she had any left. But, as the kettle finally began to boil, she discovered that she had a more than ample reserve of tears. It was like opening the floodgates. She sank forward, head resting on her arms, her body racked by uncontrollable sobs.

In the background, almost eclipsed by Lisa's anguished crying, the kettle continued its banshee wail.

Twenty

The early-morning light had trouble penetrating the layers of dirt which coated the window of the old flat. The place smelt damp despite the incessant sunshine which had bathed London and the entire country for almost three months.

Situated in Dean Street, the flat was above a disused Chinese take-away, accessible only via a rusty fire-escape at the rear of the building, but that had presented no obstacle to Steve Pollack and his companion when they had first found the empty dwelling. They had been squatting there for over a week now. Pollack guessed that the place couldn't have been empty for more than a few weeks. There was still running water from the taps in the kitchen and the toilet still flushed. When that packed up it would be time to move on and find something else.

Pollack was approaching his twenty-fourth birthday. What little time he'd had outside of reform schools, borstals or prison had been spent squatting in a succession of London's many empty buildings. His father had thrown him out when he was fifteen after discovering that Steve had taken to dipping into the old man's pockets for a quid or two when he was short of fags. He'd left without a row. As he'd said at the time, he had nothing worth staying at home for anyway. Within a week of being out on the streets he'd been arrested joyriding in a stolen car and given six months at a borstal in Oxford.

It was during his stay there that he'd met Bill Lawrence.

Lawrence was two years older than Pollack. The two of them had been inseparable since that first meeting, except for the occasions when they'd been banged up in different places. Now, with Lawrence's girlfriend Michelle in tow, they moved around together. Stealing, begging and anything else they could do to keep themselves in money. For a time Michelle had even gone on the game, bringing home anything up to fifty or sixty quid a night. This had been an easy time for Pollack and Lawrence, but after one punter beat her up in an effort to get his rocks off, Lawrence had decided that the three of them would find some other way to get cash. He'd managed to find a reliable fence who handled their stolen goods for them for a reasonable percentage. Some of the stuff they kept for themselves. Like the radio-cassette that Pollack now fiddled with, trying to find Radio One. He had knocked it off from an electrical store in Charing Cross Road only two days before. The manager of the shop had chased him but Pollack had bolted down the nearest subway and eluded the man in the crowds. He smiled at the recollection, turning the frequency knob until he found the station he sought, then he increased the volume slightly.

Moving to the window, he peered out through the film of grime, spitting on the glass and rubbing to make a clear spot. Perspiration glistened on his naked body, and from behind him he could hear the groans of pleasure from Michelle and Lawrence as they made love. Pollack turned to watch for a moment, his penis hardening as he enjoyed the spectacle of Michelle grinding herself hard onto Lawrence's own erection. She looked over to Pollack and smiled, her long hair, matted with sweat, swishing back and forth across her face as she bounced up and down. She was twenty-one but looked almost ten years older. Her body, though slim, was scarred in a number of places, her face pockmarked.

Pollack moved closer, his eyes fixed on her large breasts and swollen nipples.

'Come on Steve,' Lawrence said to him, reaching up to grab her bouncing breasts in his rough hands. 'There's plenty for both of us.' He smiled broadly.

'I'm going to have a piss,' Pollack informed him and padded across the bare floor towards the toilet. He passed through the kitchen with its cracked enamel sink, now scarred with mould. Past the small calor gas cooker which they used to heat up the tinned food. Cans both unopened and empty lay in an untidy pile on the floor nearby. There were a number of flies buzzing around the open ones, or crawling over the remnants of the food.

Pollack found some of the insects in the toilet as well, one of them crawling up the side of the pan. He stood there grinning, directing a stream of urine at the fly, which quickly flew off. With a grunt of annoyance, he looked down to see that water was seeping around his feet. The porcelain was cracked badly in a couple of places and moisture was dripping out. When he'd finished he didn't bother flushing for fear of causing the whole pan to give way. Drying his feet with a piece of toilet paper, he made his way back to the other room.

The first two slugs slithered up the side of the toilet, their forward tubercles extending as they broke the surface. Leaving a trail of thick slime behind them, the large black creatures moved upwards, followed by more of their companions, until finally the toilet was full of them and they started to overflow onto the floor, landing in a reeking pile, slithering over each other in their eagerness to reach the source of food which they knew was very close.

Michelle was on her knees, her pert bottom waving about invitingly, her slippery cleft exposed for the pleasure of the two men. Lawrence guided his throbbing member into her, gripping her hips, pulling her onto him. She squealed with pleasure as she felt the penetration.

Kneeling in front of her, Pollack nodded approvingly as she reached out and closed one hand around his penis, moving it up and down in time to Lawrence's deep thrusts. With her other hand she cupped Pollack's testicles, massaging them until she felt them tighten. Smiling, Michelle lowered her head and planted her lips around the bulbous head of his penis, moving her head up and down. Pollack felt her hair flicking over his groin and it added to his pleasure. He reached out and held her breasts, thumbing the erect nipples until they grew even stiffer. He looked up to see Lawrence pounding relentlessly into her, his own body now sheathed in perspiration.

The slithering carpet of slugs oozed beneath the toilet door like a spillage of oil, moving inexorably towards the three figures ahead of them.

Pollack closed his eyes as he felt the sensations of pleasure increasing. Michelle's head bobbed up and down more rapidly now, her tongue exploring every inch of his shaft, flicking at the moisture which oozed from the tip. He gripped her breasts tighter but the rough treatment seemed to inflame her passion and she sucked harder realizing that his climax was not far off. Nor was her own. She squirmed as she felt Lawrence slip one hand between her legs, his probing fingers searching out her swollen clitoris. He rubbed his index finger along her wet and puffy outer lips, lubricating the digit before he began rubbing in a circular motion on that most delicate spot.

The leading slugs, by now, were actually in the room, moving towards the entangled humans, sensing the warmth of their flesh and blood. As they approached, sliding over each other in their haste, they produced a vile sucking sound but their intended victims did not hear it.

More, many more, crawled up from the lavatory to join their companions.

Michelle was going to come and she closed her eyes as the enveloping feeling of warmth began to spread from her thighs and vagina to her breasts and stomach, wrapping her in what felt like a warm blanket. She pulled her mouth away from Pollack's erection long enough to gasp her pleasure, her hand now moving furiously up and down his glistening shaft until he thrust it forward towards her open mouth. She smiled as she watched the thick white fluid spurting forth, and immediately lowered her head again to catch and swallow the remaining liquid, twisting her tongue around the swollen head to lick it clean.

A second later she almost screamed with pleasure as she felt Lawrence climax inside her, his own organ filling her with ejaculate, some of which dribbled warmly down the inside of her thighs.

Pollack opened his eyes.

'Oh Jesus Christ!' he exclaimed almost falling backwards.

The room was half full of gigantic slugs. A black, glistening wall of them faced him as if they had risen from the very floorboards.

Lawrence, still trying to regain his senses after the intensity of his orgasm, was the first to feel pain as three of them bit into his calf. He pulled away from Michelle, his penis slipping out of her.

He overbalanced and rolled amongst the seething mass of slugs.

They moved with surprising speed, sliding up onto his chest and belly, digging deep into him with their sickle-like teeth, burrowing hungrily into flesh and muscle. Shrieking in pain and terror, Lawrence tried to rise but the weight of the black monstrosities held him down and all he could do was crawl, dozens of them covering him. Blood from numerous wounds mingled with the vile slime which the slugs exuded and it dripped from him like wax from a melting candle.

'Help me,' he shrieked. 'For fuck's sake help me.'

But Pollack could only stand and watch as his friend raised a hand which was itself already eaten almost to the bone by the slugs which clung to it.

Michelle was also screaming. She bolted for the door which led to the fire escape.

Their only way out.

As she ran she felt numerous slug bodies bursting beneath her feet, others bit into her toes. One particularly large creature, close to nine inches in length, managed to drive its central tooth into her ankle just below the bone. The sudden pain, coupled with the slippery floor, caused her to overbalance and she fell heavily, trying to tug the recalcitrant beast from her foot. Blood jetted onto her hands and she found that she could not get a grip on the black beast because of the foul-smelling slime which it exuded. Others now fastened themselves onto her thighs and buttocks and began eating. Michelle was screaming uncontrollably as the pain grew more intense and she felt the oblivion of unconsciousness beginning to drift over her. But she was denied that mercy when another of the larger beasts slithered up her belly and began eating her left nipple, digging deeper until it was feeding on the soft meat of her breast. The unbelievable pain prevented her from blacking out.

Blood soon covered the room as if sprayed from a hosepipe and Pollack sank almost resignedly to his haunches in one corner of the room, his eyes bulging wide with terror as he watched the remains of his two companions being devoured by the black horrors. Tears began to course down his cheeks. Tears, at first, of fear but then he began to laugh insanely. For that was all he could think to do. What he was witnessing was a dream, a vile corrupted nightmare. It had to be. Nothing like this could really happen.

He watched as the slugs seethed over the ruined bodies, sometimes emerging from *inside* the corpse, having eaten their way out. He saw the blood. He smelt the choking odour which they gave off, he sniffed the rancid smell of excrement.

Yes, this had to be a nightmare, he thought, still laughing.

The slugs drew closer, encircling him, filling the room until all he could see was an undulating black carpet of glistening bodies, bloated and yet still hungry.

He drew his knees up to his chest as the slugs moved in.

He didn't attempt to move.

A song played on the radio called 'Two Minutes to Midnight'.

It seemed most appropriate.

Pollack began to laugh even louder.

He was still laughing when the first of the slugs reached him.

Twenty-one

By the time Alan Finch reached his home in Westbourne Terrace he could hardly keep his eyes open. He checked his watch, then the clock on the mantlepiece, and saw to his disappointment that it was almost 7.06 a.m. There seemed little point in going to bed now. By the same token, there seemed even less point in attending surgery. In his state of exhaustion he would be a positive liability to his patients. Although he knew his appointment book was full he decided to ring in later and tell June that he wouldn't be in. His colleagues could cope with the extra work-load for one day.

The armchair looked inviting and the thought of his bed even more so, but instead he went to the kitchen and filled the kettle for coffee. It would be another hour before he could contact the surgery, and as tired as he felt, he dared not sit down in case he nodded off. So instead he made his way wearily up the stairs to the bathroom. There he splashed his face with cold water in an effort to banish some of the dullness from his mind. He leant on the edges of the sink studying his reflection, looking at the dark rings beneath his eyes. Caused by lack of sleep and also by the horrors he had witnessed that night. Even the warm early-morning sunshine seemed incapable of banishing the chill he felt as he thought about Mark Franklin and his dead parents. Or Molly Foster and the murdered nurse.

Or of how many others might be afflicted by this mysterious disease.

He thought briefly of Lisa and then, pushing the thoughts to the back of his mind, he splashed his face with more cold water until his skin was almost numb.

The phone rang.

Snatching up a towel, Finch headed for the bedroom.

'Doctor Alan Finch,' he said, wedging the receiver between his ear and shoulder while he dabbed away the last of the water.

'Finch, I need to speak to you in person. Now.'

He recognized the voice immediately.

'Bennett. What is it?' the doctor asked.

'Can you get to my laboratory immediately?' the pathologist wanted to know.

Before Finch had a chance to protest the other man continued.

'It's important,' he urged. 'There's something you must see.'

The doctor exhaled deeply. He decided not to mention that he'd been up since three that morning, that he'd seen another victim of this strange and deadly plague, that . . .

'Finch, did you hear what I said?' Bennett asked, agitatedly.

'I'll be there as soon as I can.'

Bennett hung up.

'Something you must see,' Finch repeated, replacing the phone on its cradle. He left the towel in the bedroom, took the time to pull on a clean shirt and trousers, then hurried downstairs to switch the kettle off.

Another five minutes and he was on his way to New Scotland Yard.

When Finch entered the lab he found Bennett perched on a stool beside one of the work-benches eating a sandwich. He nodded a greeting to the young doctor, put his sandwich down and got off his stool. Finch noticed how pale and drawn the pathologist looked.

'You look like death warmed up,' Finch said.

'Coming from you that's quite a compliment,' the pathologist told him. '*You* don't exactly look ready to run a marathon.'

117

The doctor explained briefly what had happened after he had left Bennett earlier that morning.

The pathologist nodded intently as Finch spoke about the death of Molly Foster, then he guided the younger man to a microscope which had already been set up, the slide prepared. Finch peered through the lens.

'My God,' he whispered.

On the slide before him were more of the blood flukes he'd now come to recognize so well. But they were much larger.

'That's from the same section of brain we looked at earlier,' Bennett told him. 'They've more than doubled their size and numbers in less than six hours. But that's not all.' He turned away from the microscope, back towards the stainless steel slab where the body of Mark Franklin still lay, the feet and fingers now stiff with rigor mortis. Bennett pulled back the sheet to expose the head. He had replaced the top of the cranium, shielding the brain, but now he carefully removed it once more so that Finch was able to see the contents of the skull.

'What the hell are those?' he asked, softly, indicating several growths the size of a man's thumbnail which had appeared on the crinkly surface of the cerebral cortex.

'After you left,' Bennett told him. 'I tried to figure out how blood flukes from an animal could have got into a human being's bloodstream and, more to the point, how they could have caused the damage they did. Now I know. I also know the animal they belong to.'

Finch frowned, then stood back as the pathologist took a scalpel and carefully cut round one of the growths, pulling away a small portion of brain with it. The lumps looked like polyps – small bulges which sometimes occur in the vagina or the anus. Only these were darker, like clots of congealed blood. Bennett transferred the severed growth to a Petri dish, then placed the dish on the worktop.

'It looks like some form of cyst,' Finch observed.

'It is,' the pathologist told him, his eyes never leaving the dark lump. 'It appeared about two hours ago, growing inside the brain, like the others.'

'I don't see what this has to do with the blood flukes,' Finch said, noticing that Bennett's attention seemed riveted to the revolting object which lay in the dish before them.

'The flukes *formed* those cysts,' the pathologist told him, flatly. 'The easiest comparison I can quote you is that of an amoeba. When conditions are unfavourable for an amoeba or most other single-celled animals, they have the ability to encyst. To convert themselves into cysts by forming a tougher outer covering of tissue. That's what these blood flukes are doing except that, in this case, they also undergo a metamorphosis.'

'You're telling me they can change their cellular structure?' Finch said.

Bennett nodded, his eyes still fixed on the cyst in the dish.

'You said you knew which animals they came from,' the doctor persisted. '*How* do you know?'

As if in answer to his question, Finch saw that the lump in the dish was beginning to split open. Like some small, overripe bursting plum it spilled its contents into the dish. Finch saw several small shapes slithering about in the dark liquid.

'Slugs?' he gasped, incredulously.

The creatures were barely 5mm long, but their shape was unmistakable. As he and Bennett watched, the newly hatched slugs began feeding on the fragment of brain to which the cyst had been attached.

'The flukes get into the bloodstream by penetrating the skin,' Bennett explained. 'That's the usual form of transmission. Once inside they reach maturity, grow and form cysts like those in the boy's brain. The lesions and boils on the skin are also full of the blood flukes. Inside those cysts the metamorphosis takes place. The slugs hatch and use the host as a source of food, growing all the time.'

'My God, they use their victims like incubators,' said Finch, looking with distaste at the half a dozen or so slugs which had emerged from the crimson swelling and were devouring the portion of brain. 'Some spiders and wasps use the same method, don't they? The eggs are laid inside the host, then there's a ready-made food supply waiting for the young.'

'That's exactly what we've got here,' Bennett said.

'So the boy and Molly Franklin were in contact with slugs?' Finch said, his voice low.

'The flukes travel in the slime trails which the slugs leave behind. These two victims must have touched that slime. It permeated their skin.'

The doctor took a scalpel and carefully eased it under one of the pale creatures in the Petri dish. It was a sickly white, yet to attain its mature black colour. The small body was stained with crimson and, as Finch looked at it, he saw its eye stalks extending like twin aerials.

Bennett crossed the lab to a cupboard, retrieved a large glass jar and returned to join Finch. The pathologist held up the jar, revealing the contents.

Slithering around inside were a dozen or more slugs, slipping and sliding over each other, some nudging at the lid of the jar. Not one was less than two inches long. Thick and black, they looked like severed, re-animated fingers.

'These hatched four hours ago,' said Bennett, flatly. 'From the size of a thumbnail to two inches in such a short time. It's incredible.'

Finch didn't answer. He took one last look at the slugs in the jar, then pulled on his jacket.

'Where are you going?' Bennett wanted to know.

But Finch was already half-way out of the door.

The pathologist gazed in at the slithering black creatures, wondering where the hell Finch had dashed off to, also wondering how he was going to explain his findings to Detective Inspector Grogan. Then he looked again at the smaller slugs, which continued to feed on the portion of Mark Franklin's brain.

It took Finch some time to convince the morgue assistant at the Middlesex Hospital that he should be allowed to see the body of Molly Foster.

'You're not a relative, are you?' the man said, picking a

piece of food from between his dirty, protruding front teeth.

'No, I told you, I'm her doctor,' Finch said.

'You're a bit late to help her, aren't you?' the man chuckled humourlessly. 'She's been in the freezers for over two hours.' The man eyed Finch suspiciously for a moment and then finally relented, leading him down to the morgue.

'The coroner isn't arriving until later this morning,' he said. 'I don't think he's going to be too happy if he knows someone's been fiddling around with one of his stiffs. If you get my meaning?'

'Just let me see the body,' snapped Finch, irritably.

The man held up both hands in a gesture of placation, then he turned and found the appropriate door. Finch stood by expectantly as the drawer was pulled out.

He recoiled from the vile stench which rose from the metal coffin but it was the morgue attendant who spoke first.

'What the fuck is this?' he gasped.

Where the body of Molly Foster had been only a short time before, there now remained only a bloodied mess of bones and wasted flesh. The face, including the eyes, had been completely stripped of flesh as had the neck and most of the upper torso. Congealed blood coated the corpse, mingling with thick slime to form a sheath. Finch saw some of the oozing fluid dripping in heavy globules from one exposed rib. The cabinet itself was full of the slime too, gleaming with a vile lustre beneath the powerful fluorescents.

The attendant reached out towards the glistening mess but Finch grabbed his wrist.

'Don't touch it,' he snapped, unable to take his eyes from the remains of the body.

It was only when he stepped back that he noticed a number of mucus trails leading from the cabinet, across the floor to a drain which lay close to one of the stainless steel slabs. The silvery paths had hardened and crusted over, like a scab over a cut.

There was no sign of the slugs.

Saturday – the 15th

Twenty-two

It looked more like a blue-print for a computer than a map of London's sewer system.

The large piece of paper was laid out on the polished oak table and held down at each corner by the weight of an ashtray.

Donald Robertson stubbed out his cigarette in one of the crystal dishes and immediately lit another. He regarded the map warily, peering at the dozen or so red crosses marked on it. His left eye twitched for a moment, as it had a habit of doing when he was worried or annoyed. He'd been head of the Thames Water Central Division for the past eighteen months, but this was his first major problem. There'd been the incident about six months ago when one of the old sewers had caved in, trapping three maintenance men for a couple of hours, but nothing on the scale of what he was facing at the moment.

He peered at the map once again, his eye twitching almost in time to his pulse.

'Soho, St. Giles, Piccadilly and Bloomsbury,' he said, tapping the map with the end of his pen. 'All the complaints have come from that area.' He drew a circle around it. 'If this goes on much longer we'll have the Department of the Environment banging on the bloody door wanting to know what's going on.'

'It's pretty obvious, Don,' said the second man in the room. He had yet to reach forty, a year or so younger than Robertson. He wore a dark blue suit which was badly in need of pressing. The collar points of his shirt were curled upward like dead leaves, looking as though they might poke his eyes out if he bent forward too quickly. 'One of the filters is blocked,' he continued.

'Well, that's your responsibility, Ed,' Robertson told him, his eye twitching madly. 'I thought the bloody things were checked out regularly.'

'They are,' Edward Dowd assured him. 'Every filter is inspected and cleaned at least three times a week.'

The third man in the room stepped forward and ran his finger over the map. Max Kelly was a tall, powerfully built man with arms like tree-trunks and hands the size of hamhocks. His head, on the other hand, balding and bearing a pair of heavy-lensed glasses, looked as if it belonged to someone else, perhaps the unfortunate result of a misconceived transplant. He had the body of a lumberjack and the head of a cartoon boffin.

'It must be one hell of a blockage to cause the problems we've been notified of,' he said.

'Some of the sewers around that area are pretty old, it could be that there's been a collapse,' Dowd offered.

Robertson began pacing the floor agitatedly, drawing hard on his cigarette.

'Toilets won't flush,' he snapped. 'Effluent can't be disposed of and there's even been raw sewage coming up into the streets in a couple of places. I've got a letter here from some bloke who went down to his cellar for something and the poor sod nearly drowned in sh . . . in waste. It had come up through his floor.'

'I'll get a team of maintenance men down there straight away,' Kelly said.

'I can't understand why all this has started happening so suddenly,' Robertson said irritably. He looked at Dowd. 'And before you say anything, Ed, I don't think a collapse would cause this amount of damage. I'm sticking with the filters.'

'I'm not arguing with you, Don,' the other man said. 'I just *suggested* it might be a tunnel collapse.'

'Well, whatever it is, I want it cleared fast. I don't have to tell either of you about the health risks from something like this.'

The three men looked at each other, then at the map with its profusion of red crosses.

'If we don't get something done quick,' added Robertson, taking a final puff on his cigarette, 'we'll have all kinds of diseases in the city. I think the first plague of London was enough, don't you?'

Whether his remark was intended to be humorous or not the other men didn't know.

Either way, no one laughed.

In two streets just off New Oxford Street, raw sewage oozed up from the drains and spilled into the road. The stench, intensified by the blistering heat, was unbelievable.

A number of office buildings had to be evacuated when toilets overflowed, spilling waste everywhere.

A hotel in Shaftesbury Avenue received complaints from a number of its guests when they found puddles of partially diluted human waste seeping beneath the doors of their rooms.

The courtyard of the British Museum was flooded by gallons of reeking water which bubbled from a drain.

A group of tourists visiting the waxwork display in The Palladium Cellars were shocked to find that they were rapidly being engulfed by stinking water which rose up to their ankles in only a minute or two.

A number of stations on the Central, Northern and Piccadilly lines found that sewage was beginning to form pools beneath the electrified tracks.

By 2.00 p.m. the situation was all but out of control.

Twenty-three

'Slugs?'

Detective Inspector Ray Grogan shook his head incredulously, then looked again at the jar, which now seemed to be full of twisting, writhing black shapes.

'You're trying to tell me that the tramp we found chewed up in Leicester Square and that sewer bloke we dragged out of the pipe near the Thames were killed by *slugs*?'

'I found it as hard to believe as you, Ray,' Bennett confessed.

'You mean slugs like you find in your garden?'

'Do these look like the type you'd find in your garden?' Bennett asked, holding up the jar. 'They're hybrids. Somewhere along the way they interbred, maybe with some carnivorous species, perhaps even with another gastropod like a leech. I don't know. What I do know is that we've got one hell of a problem on our hands.'

'Make that two problems,' Grogan said. 'There's been a foul-up in one or more of the sewer tunnels under central London. I just heard from the Water Board. The streets are going to be full of shit in a few hours and now you're trying to tell me I've got an army of man-eating slugs roaming around.' He lit up a cigarette. 'What the fuck do you take me for, George? Do I look like a twat? Slugs that eat people! Do me a favour.'

'We found no traces of a murder weapon having been used on either the tramp or the sewer man,' Bennett persisted. 'But I found secretions on both bodies which carry the same type of blood flukes that infected Mark Franklin and Molly

128

Foster.' The pathologist looked at Grogan's cigarette. 'By the way, don't smoke in here, please.'

The two men, along with Finch and DS Nicholson, were seated around one of the workbenches in the laboratory. Bennett had just finished his explanations of what he and Finch had discovered earlier that day.

'You reckon that both the lad and the old girl came into contact with these slugs,' Nicholson said to Finch. 'How come they weren't eaten?'

'They didn't come into direct contact with the slugs, only the slime trails they'd left behind,' Finch corrected him.

'Assuming that's true,' Grogan interjected, 'if this disease is passed on by touching the slime, why didn't Bennett catch it? He examined both victims who'd supposedly been "eaten".' The DI tried to disguise the scorn in his voice but couldn't quite manage it.

'I was wearing gloves on both occasions,' the pathologist explained. 'For the slime to have effect it must come into *direct* contact with the skin.'

'Also, there's every reason to believe that it loses its potency after a certain time,' Finch added.

'So anyone coming into contact with these bloody things has got two ways to go. They either get eaten or they catch this disease. Right?' said the DI.

'They end up as food eventually, anyway,' Finch said.

'Oh of course, I forgot about the eggs hatching out inside them,' Grogan said, disdainfully.

'Not eggs, cysts,' Bennett insisted. 'Look, Ray, you can be as sceptical as you like, the evidence is here in front of us. The two men that were found were devoured by slugs. Both Molly Foster *and* Mark Franklin contracted a disease transmitted by those same slugs.'

'Christ, and I had a salad for lunch,' said Nicholson, chuckling.

'It's not funny,' the pathologist snapped. 'If the slugs *are* using the sewers to move around in, then all that sewage that's flooding the streets will be contaminated with the same disease. God knows how many more people will be infected.'

An awkward silence descended, finally broken by Finch.

'Slugs give off what's called a repugnatorial secretion,' he began. 'It's formed by certain cells which they utilise to form the mucus trails. The sewers must be full of it, and now it's getting into people's homes as well.'

Grogan looked at the jar full of black slugs and chewed his lip contemplatively.

'Let's just say for a minute that I accept what you're both saying.' He exhaled. 'How in God's name can a man be eaten by slugs? It's not as if you can't outrun the bloody things, is it?' He smiled thinly.

'There must be thousands of them by now,' said Bennett. 'It wouldn't be a case of outrunning then. They'd overwhelm their prey by weight of numbers. And size too.' He raised his eyebrows.

'*Giant* slugs?' Grogan shook his head. 'No, sorry, George but I'm not swallowing that. You'll be asking me to believe in Father Christmas next.' He reached for another cigarette, stuck it in his mouth, but didn't light up.

'Not giants, just large ones,' Bennett said. 'It's like the goldfish-bowl theory. If you put a goldfish in a small bowl it'll stay small because there's no room for it to grow. The principle is the same with these slugs. If they're using the sewer tunnels to breed then that gives them much more room not only to multiply but also to increase in size. Maybe the heat wave makes a difference too. They've got a combination of the perfect breeding ground and heat like a tropical jungle.' He pointed to the monstrosities in the jar. 'These are twice the size of common slugs and they've got that way in a third of the normal time. They begin growing as soon as they emerge from the cysts; the growth rate is phenomenal.'

'So what do we do?' Nicholson asked, some of the lightness now gone from his tone. 'We have to warn people.'

Grogan held up a hand.

'We still don't have any concrete proof,' he said. 'If we announce your ... *findings*, then people are going to panic.' Again Finch caught that slight hint of mockery in the policeman's voice, although this time, to a certain extent, it was tempered by caution. 'And that's just for starters,' Grogan went on. 'The other thing that bothers me is, if you're wrong, I personally don't fancy trying to explain to the commissioner that we made a balls-up. If I mention man-eating slugs to him I'll be walking the beat again.' He sighed. 'Just let it rest for a day or two...'

Finch interrupted.

'We don't *have* a day or two,' he snapped. 'It's just one area of London at the moment, in two or three days it could be the whole city.'

'How do you know it's only one area?' Grogan demanded.

'Molly Foster and Mark Franklin lived close together. The tramp you found was discovered in Leicester Square, the sewer man was washed out of that pipe near Westminster bridge. The incidents have a pattern to them.'

The DI shifted the unlit cigarette from one side of his mouth to the other.

'Whereabouts is the sewage leaking? Which streets?' the doctor persisted.

'All over the bloody West End from what the Water Board told me,' Grogan admitted. 'It's worse in some places than others of course.'

'What is the Water Board doing about it?' Bennett enquired.

'They're sending teams of engineers down to find out what's causing the blockage and clear it.'

'Well, let's hope they find the answer quickly,' Finch said. 'Because if that sewage continues pouring into the streets we're going to have an epidemic on our hands.'

'With this heat too, there's a risk of more conventional diseases breaking out, like cholera or typhus,' the pathologist put in.

Grogan massaged the bridge of his nose between thumb and forefinger.

'Flesh-eating slugs, typhus, cholera and a disease that turns people into raving maniacs,' he sighed. 'Does someone want to give me some *good* news?'

Twenty-four

The traffic cones had been placed close together at either end of Bucknall Street and a number of policemen stood or walked back and forth in front of the cordons, ensuring that interested onlookers didn't begin to form a crowd, and also directing the diverted stream of cars, buses and lorries which found the thoroughfare closed.

As the afternoon sun continued to blaze relentlessly in the cloudless sky, more than one of the uniformed men found perspiration soaking through his shirt. The men were thankful that they had been allowed to remove their tunics, but that seemed to help little as the humid heat covered the city like a suffocating blanket.

The heat alone would have been bad enough, but they also had to contend with the stench which filled their nostrils at every turn.

The street was flooded to a depth of at least three inches with vile-smelling brown water which had poured out of the drains and spread across the tarmac like ink soaking into blotting paper. Some of the more solid matter amidst the liquid was beginning to bake hard beneath the merciless sun, and most of the policemen did their best not to look at the muck which had been spewed forth.

Parked inside the cordon was a large transit van which bore the legend THAMES WATER AUTHORITY on both sides.

It was from this van that the four engineers had emerged who now stood around the manhole in the centre of the road, looking down into the murky depths. One of them, holding a

132

plan of the sewer tunnels, pointed to the spot on the map which marked the manhole around which they were gathered.

'The water level's receded since we were first called,' Max Kelly said, shining his torch down into the hole. A long way down it glinted on the surface of the water. 'See if the others are down yet,' he told a man on his left.

The man plucked a two-way radio from his belt, fiddled with the controls and pressed the set to his ear, ignoring the violent hiss of static which erupted from the hand-set.

'Atkins, come in, please,' the man said. 'Can you hear me, Terry? This is Irvine.'

There was another crackle of static.

'Yeah, I hear you,' a metallic voice answered.

'Are you down yet?' Irvine wanted to know.

'We're on our way. What about you?'

'Likewise.'

Kelly held out his hand and took the two-way from Irvine.

'Atkins, it's Max Kelly. What are the conditions like where you are?'

There was a moment's silence, as if Atkins were considering his answer. Then he spoke again:

'Well, the street's flooded but I don't know about down below. I think the water level's dropped but we don't know for sure until we get down into the tunnels.'

Kelly signed off, reminding Atkins to get in touch if he discovered the problem. The second team of engineers were in Wardour Street, less than a mile away.

'This is a low-level intercepting sewer according to these plans,' Kelly said, pointing at the manhole. 'We should be able to move through without too much trouble.' He turned once more to the man on his left. 'Irvine, you stay up here. The rest of us will go down,' he motioned to the other two men with him. 'Keep in contact with us and with Atkins' crew, right?'

Irvine nodded, watching the first man swing himself down into the manhole and catch hold of the metal ladder which disappeared into the blackness below.

He began to descend, followed by the next engineer, then

finally by Kelly himself, who checked his safety lamp briefly before clambering down the ladder. With such an apparently large overflow all the men were aware that there was much more danger of gas pockets.

As they climbed deeper into the enveloping gloom the leading engineer, a tall, red-haired man named Hamilton, flicked on his torch and stuck it in his belt. He heard the sound of water slapping lazily against the walls of the tunnel, and a moment later his foot was immersed in the reeking brown fluid. He descended further, the river of effluent reaching his knees, then his thighs. With a shiver he felt it spill over the top of his waders, soaking into his overalls. Hamilton paused, his foot on the bottom rung of the ladder. The water should have been no higher than his thighs but it was already sloshing around his waist. He pulled the torch from his belt and shone it around the tunnel.

Even the walls and roof were dripping. The water had, at some time earlier, filled the tunnel completely. And, he thought with a shudder, there was no guarantee that it would not happen again. Gritting his teeth he stepped off the ladder and the water lapped at his chest.

'Jesus,' he called. 'It must be over five feet deep down here.'

Kelly heard the shout and steadied himself to join his two men in the chest-high muck. As he reached the bottom of the ladder he swayed uncertainly for a moment, almost slipping on the slimy ooze which clung to the tunnel floor. He relayed the information to Irvine then switched off the two-way.

The sewer tunnel curved away to the left and Kelly moved ahead, finding that it was difficult to move easily with the weight of water against him. He and the other two engineers forced their way onward through the vile discoloured liquid, trying as best they could to ignore the stench.

'Some of this lot should have run off into a storm relief outlet,' Kelly said, panting from the effort of wading through the effluent. Every so often a lump of solid waste would bump against him but he ignored it and pushed on, the torch beam cutting a swath through the gloom.

Kelly paused and held up his safety lamp, checking that there was no flicker from the red light.

So far they were still clear. The three men moved on, noticing that the tunnel was widening slightly as the curve became more pronounced.

Hamilton suddenly stopped.

'Listen,' he urged, holding up a hand.

His two companions both stopped in their tracks and cocked their ears in the direction he was pointing.

Kelly heard it too.

A series of loud splashes, and something even louder. A low sucking sound, like many feet being pulled from clinging mud.

It was coming from just ahead of them, around the curve in the tunnel.

All three men recoiled from a particularly powerful and nauseating odour. A smell so fetid that, for a second, Kelly felt as if he'd been struck physically. He coughed, trying to breathe through his mouth to minimize the effects of the choking stench. They all knew the smell of the sewers, they recognized the first tell-tale whiffs of methane and the stink of excrement and urine, but this was something else. A smell so putrid it stopped them in their tracks.

In the silence there was a sudden harsh crackle from the radio and Hamilton almost lost his footing.

Kelly grabbed the two-way and pressed it to his ear.

'What's happening?' Irvine wanted to know. 'Is everything OK?'

'We're just about to find out,' Kelly told him, rounding the corner. 'I think there could be a blockage . . .'

The words trailed off as he shone his torch around the tunnel bend, swinging the beam back and forth.

His lips moved but no sound would come forth. The radio quivered in his hand.

'Oh my God,' he whispered.

'I didn't get that,' Irvine said. 'Have you found the blockage?'

Hamilton too was standing, arms held limply at his sides,

gazing wide-eyed at the far end of the tunnel.

The third man, Turner, could only shake his head in disbelief.

'What's happening, Max?' Irvine's voice on the two-way sounded miles away.

'Oh Christ,' Kelly murmured, his mouth dropping open.

The tunnel was at least twelve feet wide, perhaps eight feet high. More like a railway tunnel than a sewer.

Every square inch of brick was covered by a seething mass of slugs.

They stretched across the tunnel and up it, their glistening black bodies catching the torch-light like obscene cat's-eyes. A wall of slimy, bloated shapes blocking the filter which Kelly knew was behind the reeking horde. It was these monstrous creatures which had caused the overflow, their hideous forms packed so tightly together that the water could find no way through.

As they slid up and over each other some fell into the filthy water and that, the men realized, what was had made the splashing sound they'd heard.

Moving slowly, as if he feared that any sudden action might cause the black mass to move, Kelly raised the two-way to his mouth.

'Call Atkins,' he said, quietly, the words almost catching in his throat. 'Tell him and his men to get out of the sewer.'

'What's wrong?' Irvine wanted to know.

'Just do it,' rasped Kelly, his eyes never leaving the slugs as they crawled and slithered, heaving their bloated bodies over the bricks and over each other, occasionally dropping into the water.

Dropping into the water.

The realization hit him like a thunderbolt and he began backing off, moving with difficulty against the swell of effluent.

'Let's get out of here,' he said, and his two companions needed no second warning. Turner, in particular, tried to turn and run but the depth and volume of the viscous liquid made that impossible. Arms flailing, he tried to push past his companions, knowing that the ladder which led to safety was no more than twenty yards away.

It might as well have been twenty miles.

Hamilton, still watching the slugs, saw one particularly large creature fall into the water, and moments later he felt something nudge against his thigh.

Sudden agonizing pain tore through him and he roared in surprise as he felt a series of stabbing motions against his leg. He thrust one hand into the water, his fingers closing over the large slug that was burrowing into his flesh. With a shriek he tore it free, holding it before him for a second, noticing with a twinge of disgust that a long streamer of skin hung from its churning mouth parts.

His skin.

He was about to hurl the monstrosity away when it suddenly twisted in his grasp and drove its sickle-shaped central tooth into the back of his hand. Blood burst from the wound but the slug tore itself free and struck again, driving its hungry mouth at the meatier part of his forearm.

Hamilton screamed again and turned to run but he overbalanced.

Kelly saw what was going to happen and pressed himself against the nearest wall.

Hamilton disappeared beneath the surface of the water. His head appeared a second later with two slugs boring into his face. He tried to scream but a third slipped inside his mouth, pressing against the back of his throat until he gagged violently.

At the same time, Turner found that half a dozen of the creatures were clinging to his back, eating their way through his overalls in an effort to reach the flesh beneath. When they finally did so his shrieks filled the cavern, bouncing off the walls until Kelly thought he would go mad.

For his own part he pressed on, noticing that more and more slugs were now dropping from the walls into the water, all eager to reach this fresh prey. He shivered with horror as he saw Turner disappear beneath the water.

Were these things slugs? he thought, immediately

answering his own question. No, it was impossible, slugs didn't eat human flesh . . .

He realized how wrong he was.

Searing agony shot through him from crotch to brain as two of them began boring into his inner thigh. He tore one free, and the second he crushed in his hand, its body fluids oozing over his fingers. A fresh stench assailed his nostrils as the slug split in two, the half he still held pulping yellowish pus-like blood everywhere. He snatched at his radio, gritting his teeth as he felt new pain in his thighs and buttocks, then the small of his back.

One of the larger creatures was eating its way through to his kidneys.

'Irvine,' he gasped. 'Get help for God's sake . . .' The pleas dissolved into shouts of pain as he felt his lower body enveloped by red-hot pain. He could actually feel blood bursting from his back. He could sense the slug digging deeper inside him.

But he struggled on, now alone in the tunnel.

Both Turner and Hamilton were gone.

'I'm coming down,' Irvine told him.

'No! Just get help.'

Blood filled his mouth and he felt himself swaying but just ahead, visible in the semi-darkness beneath the manhole, was the ladder.

His head was spinning now and he knew that he was going to fall. There was nothing he could do to stop himself. He pitched forward into the stinking water.

When he finally dragged himself upright another slug was eating into his ear. Blood was pouring down the side of his face and he was moaning gutturally, but he found the strength to wrench the creature free, ripping most of his ear away with it. His nose was full of filthy liquid, his mouth was clogged with blood, but he fought his way on until at last his hand gripped one of the ladder rungs.

'What's happening down there?'

Irvine's voice rattled from the two-way.

Kelly didn't answer. He was trying to drag himself up the

metal ladder. One of his legs dangled uselessly, eaten to the bone. The other barely supported him. Calling on all his reserves of strength he began dragging himself up, one rung at a time, aware that two or three slugs were still clinging to his body.

One was slithering up his spine towards the hollow at the base of his skull.

'Help me,' Kelly screamed, desperation giving volume to the bellow of pain and frustration.

He was less than two feet from the manhole.

The slug on the back of his neck fixed its tooth into his flesh and attacked.

The pain was so sudden and unexpectedly excruciating that he lost his grip and fell several feet. One outstretched hand gripped a rung further down and he came to a jarring halt, blood gushing from the numerous wounds on his body.

Above him, Irvine peered down into the blackness, shining his torch down onto what could have been a picture plucked from some insane horror film.

Kelly was hanging by one arm, his face was white as milk, smeared with blood and excrement, his overalls in tatters, matted and crimson. And the engineer noticed something else.

The thick black shapes that glided so easily over his companion's skin.

Kelly looked up, sensing that his grip on consciousness was fading rapidly. He tried to call out but all that came forth was a thick gout of blood, spilling over his lips and chin. With every fibre of courage and endurance left, he began to climb once more.

Irvine straightened up and yelled to the nearby policemen.

'Help me, quick,' he shouted and two of the constables hurdled the cordon of cones and came sprinting across the flooded street towards the sewer man. Together, they hauled Kelly up the last couple of feet from the black mouth of the manhole.

The last slug fell from his body and disappeared beneath the water far below.

As Kelly rolled over on the filthy pavement the full extent of his injuries was clear for the three observers to see. His eyes were bulging wide in their sockets, as if something on the inside were trying to force them out and his lips fluttered soundlessly, blood spilling from his mouth.

'I'd better get an ambulance,' said one of the policemen, hurrying away.

Kelly's body underwent a violent muscular spasm, then was still. A soft hiss signalled the collapse of his sphincter muscle.

'No need to hurry,' the other constable sighed. 'It's not an ambulance he needs now.'

The fierce sun beat down relentlessly upon the little tableau.

Detective Inspector Ray Grogan lit a cigarette and looked one last time at the body of Max Kelly. Then he nodded and the blanket was pulled back over the mutilated mass which had once been a man.

'There was slime on the corpse,' said Bennett in a weary voice, wiping a bead of perspiration from his forehead.

'What about the other men who went down there with him?' Grogan asked Irvine.

'There's been no sign of them,' the sewer man told him.

The DI sucked hard on his Marlboro. He was aware of Bennett's gaze upon him.

'And neither of you saw anything?' Grogan asked the two constables.

'No, sir,' they said in unison.

'Tell me again what *you* saw,' the DI said to Irvine.

'Like I told you,' he began. 'There were . . . *things* crawling on him. Black things.'

'*Things* is a vague word.'

'Animals of some kind, like worms only much bigger. Horrible fucking things whatever they were.'

'Slugs,' said Bennett.

'Yeah,' Irvine confirmed. 'They looked like slugs.'

Grogan took a last drag from his cigarette and dropped it to the ground, only half-smoked. It hissed angrily in the spilt water. He looked at Bennett, his face set in tight lines.

'Well, Ray,' the pathologist said. 'Do you want me to come with you when you go to see the Commissioner?'

Twenty-five

Finch couldn't remember how long he'd been sitting watching the house in Melbury Road.

He'd driven there immediately after leaving New Scotland Yard. The journey to Kensington had not been an unduly long one but it had been made more uncomfortable by the searing heat. In places, the tarmac was beginning to blister.

The street was quiet except for a couple of children squatting on the hot pavement near his car, who were amusing themselves by dropping small pebbles onto some ants which had made their nest between two paving stones. Finch sat back in his seat, feeling the perspiration soaking into his shirt. He watched the children for a moment longer, then clambered out of the car, wiping the palms of his hands on his trousers. He found that his hands were shaking slightly, but he remembered that they usually did when he stood before this particular house.

He walked swiftly up the short path and rapped three times on the front foor. There was no answer so he knocked again. After a moment or two he heard sounds of movement from inside and then the door was opened.

'Hello, Theresa,' he said, a vague smile on his face.

His ex-wife regarded him impassively. If she was surprised to see him then it certainly didn't register in her expression.

'Hello, Alan,' she said, that distinctively husky voice still as potent as ever but with no trace of emotion in it.

Finch cast her a rapid appraising glance, enough to realize that she was still as attractive as ever. Her long auburn hair was drawn up, held in position by slides. She was wearing a white T-shirt, her nipples straining darkly against the material. The faded denim skirt she wore clung tightly to her buttocks, the split in it revealing a good portion of her long, slender legs.

'What do you want?' she asked him. 'You're not supposed to pick Christopher up until tomorrow.'

'I know that.' There was an awkward silence as they looked at one another, then Finch spoke again. 'I need to talk to you. Could I come in for a minute, please?'

Theresa hesitated then stepped aside and ushered him in.

'Richard's not here at the moment anyway,' she said, closing the door behind him.

'It wasn't Richard I came to see,' Finch told her, a note of irritation in his voice. He walked through to the sitting room, welcoming its relative coolness.

'Would you like a drink?' she asked him, moving towards a cabinet on the other side of the room.

He declined at first, but when she poured herself a large scotch and soda he accepted an orange juice. Theresa handed it to him and seated herself in one of the large armchairs. Finch did likewise.

'Where's Christopher?' he asked, smiling as he saw his son's photo on the mantlepiece.

'He's at a birthday party. One of the kids he goes to school with is six today. It's over in Bloomsbury somewhere, I've got to pick him up later.'

A flicker of concern passed behind Finch's eyes but he said nothing.

'You look tired, Alan,' she told him, without the slightest hint of concern. 'Have you been overworking or is it a case of too much bed and not enough sleep?' She raised her eyebrows.

'You know better than that.'

'Of course. It might interfere with your career.' Her voice

was heavy with sarcasm.

'Theresa, I didn't come here to argue. I came here to ask you something.' He rolled the glass between his hands. 'I want you and Chris to leave London. Go today if you can, but just get out.'

Theresa paused, the glass almost touching her lips.

'I don't know what Richard will think of that,' she told him.

'I couldn't care less what Richard thinks,' Finch rasped. 'I'm asking you to do it for Christopher's sake. Isn't that enough?'

'Why do you want us to leave?'

Finch exhaled.

'I don't know all the details,' he began, wearily. 'Not yet, but I know that there's a virus of some kind spreading through the city. I've already seen a couple of cases personally and I know there'll be more.'

'What kind of virus?'

He wondered if he should mention the possible threat of the slugs but eventually decided against it.

'No one knows exactly,' he said. 'Listen, Theresa, can't you take my word for it? I wouldn't have come here if I didn't think it was important.'

'We're not married any more, Alan. I can make my own decisions.'

'I'm not telling you what to do, for Christ's sake.' His face darkened as he continued, barely able to keep his temper under control. 'Despite what's happened between us I still care about you. It might be possible for *you* to wipe out the memory of six years of marriage but I can't. I still care about you but I *love* Chris. I'm not asking you to do anything for me, I know you better than that. Do it for Chris.'

They regarded each other across the room, each one waiting for the next cutting barb. Theresa sipped her drink, watching her ex-husband over the rim of the glass.

'It's not as easy as that, Alan,' she said, her tone softening slightly. 'Despite what you may think of Richard he's still my . . .' She struggled to find the words.

'Lover,' Finch interjected. 'Don't be afraid of using the

term in front of me, Theresa. It's not as if you're telling me something I didn't already know.'

'I don't know what he'll say.'

'Well, if he won't go, then leave without him.' Now it was the doctor's turn to rely on sarcasm. 'Or if you can't bear to be without him, send Chris to me and *I'll* get him out.'

Theresa gazed into the bottom of her glass for a moment, lost in thought, then she looked Finch directly in the eye.

'What are you going to do?' she wanted to know. 'Assuming that I do take Chris out of the city. Are you leaving too?'

'I don't know,' he said. 'I think my talents would be better employed here if the virus does spread, as it seems it will.'

'The good doctor will always be on hand. Right?' The fire had returned to her voice.

Finch got to his feet.

'I've already said my piece,' he announced. 'Please do what I've asked. You owe it to Chris.'

Her eyes narrowed to tiny slits.

'I don't owe Chris anything,' she hissed. 'I've given him more love in the last six years than any child has a right to expect so don't tell me I *owe* it to him.'

'Then you'll take him out of London?' said Finch.

Theresa didn't answer, she merely swallowed what was left in her glass, then got to her feet, crossed to the drinks cabinet and poured another large measure of scotch.

From the direction of the hall they both heard a key being turned in the lock, and a moment later, Richard Crane entered the sitting room. He looked at Finch, then at Theresa, then back at Finch again.

'Hello, Alan,' he said.

'It's all right, Richard, I was just leaving,' the doctor told him, heading towards the hall. He turned as he reached it, his face focussing on his ex-wife.

'Remember what I've said,' he asked. Then he was gone. He closed the front door behind him and walked back down the path, past the two kids who were still bombarding ants with stones, back to his car. Finch slid behind the wheel and twisted the key in the ignition. He took a final look at the house, then drove off.

Twenty-six

Carol Mendham, turned away coughing, unable to take any more of the vile fumes rising from the blocked toilet. She pushed the bathroom window further open, stuck her head out and sucked in several lungfuls of clean air. There might not be any cooling breeze but it was better than bending over the reeking bowl. As the evening approached slowly, almost tentatively, the sun lost some of its potency. Sinking low in the sky it glowed brilliant blood red, like some kind of huge warning flare, giving notice that the next day would bring no respite from the soaring temperatures.

Carol pulled off her rubber gloves, took one last defiant look at the blocked lavatory, then threw the garments into the nearby waste-bin. She washed her hands thoroughly, muttering to herself when she saw a red mark on the back of her left hand. Peering more closely at it, she saw that it looked like a heat bump. No wonder in this weather, she thought, rinsing the soap off. The damn thing itched too.

There was another on her forearm and one, slightly larger, on her wrist. She dried her hands and reached into the medicine cabinet on the bathroom wall, searching through the contents for the calamine lotion. As she opened the door she caught sight of her own reflection and was surprised to see how pale she looked.

What was more, she noted with annoyance, there was another of those blasted bumps on her forehead.

Carol found the calamine and dabbed it on; she had to tilt

her head to get a proper look in the mirror. She smiled to herself. The cabinet was on a slant. She'd told Hugh when he'd put it up that it wasn't straight but he would hear none of it. He could learn anything from a book, he'd told her, so with the Do-It-Yourself manual open in front of him and his tools laid out like a surgeon's implements, he'd set to work. The lop-sided cabinet was only one of his 'triumphs'. She'd lived with Hugh Francis for over nine months now, and in that time she had learned that his attempts at DIY were positively lethal. The sort of bloke who changes plugs with a hammer, her father called him. The thought of plugs brought back memories of the time he'd tried to wire up the new video and managed to fuse the lights in the whole block.

Carol looked back at the toilet and wished that he really did have a knack for household repairs, particularly plumbing.

It had been blocked for nearly a day now. They'd emptied buckets of water into it to disperse some of the waste, but with only limited success. Carol had scrabbled around trying to locate the blockage, but she had not discovered one. Other flats in the block, she knew, were suffering similar problems with their water works, and she'd heard on the news that some streets nearby had been flooded.

She made her way along the hall, the smell of food greeting her as she entered the kitchen. Carol felt her stomach contract despite the appetizing aromas and, for one second, she thought she was going to be sick. But the feeling passed and she didn't say anything.

Hugh was standing by the oven door, a towel wrapped around each hand, pulling a deep dish from inside the oven. He wore only a pair of jeans, but perspiration was rolling off his back. As Carol entered the room he turned and placed the joint of beef on a plate.

'A roast on Saturday evenings,' she said. 'People will think we're rolling in it.'

'Well, if we can't celebrate my appointment to a Fleet Street newspaper in style then I think there's something wrong,' Hugh told her.

He'd been a free-lance journalist for the past four years but lately one of the Fleet Street tabloids had published his work on such a regular basis that they had decided to offer him a full-time position. Hence the celebration.

He stood over the joint, the electric carving knife in his hand, carefully and effortlessly slicing off portions of the meat. Carol sat back in the chair watching him, becoming aware of a dull ache building slowly at the back of her neck.

'Are you feeling OK, love?' he asked.

She nodded.

'If the toilet's still blocked on Monday I'll give the water authorities another call,' he said, carving the last of the meat and laying the knife down. He turned towards the fridge and pulled out a bottle of red wine.

'Mustn't forget the *vino*,' he said, chuckling. 'It's a pity it's not champagne . . .'

He heard the loud clatter of the electric carving knife behind him, building to a muted roar as the blades moved back and forth with dizzying speed.

The smile on Hugh's face faded as he turned round and saw Carol holding it before her, her features twisted into a grimace.

She drove the knife forward, using both hands to push it further. The rapidly moving twin blades effortlessly slashed through the muscles of Hugh's stomach before churning on into his intestines. He screamed and dropped the wine bottle which shattered, the alcohol mingling with his own blood which was now gushing freely from the hideous rent in his belly.

He fell, trying to push Carol away, his eyes bulging wide in pain and terror as he saw severed lengths of intestine bulging through the massive cut.

Hugh raised his hand to ward her off but she sliced off two of his fingers with the lethal implement, sweeping it downwards so that the serrated blades powered into his neck at the point where it joined his shoulder. A huge fountain of crimson erupted from the cut, splattering Carol who kept both blood-drenched hands on the electric knife, moving it back and forth in a sawing motion which threatened to sever

Hugh's head. His head lolled backwards at an impossible angle as she cut through his windpipe, the blades grating against, then pulverising, his larynx. Pieces of skin flew into the air like grisly confetti and only when she was too exhausted to hold onto the knife any longer did Carol finally switch it off.

In the relative silence which followed, she slumped back, staring blankly at the mutilated corpse, feeling the blood soaking into her clothes.

As it dripped from the walls it sounded as if the kitchen had a faulty tap.

David Maguire sat on the edge of the bed and carefully put his weight on first his left foot then his right.

He hissed in pain each time.

The blisters on the soles of his feet made the act painful in the extreme. Walking was almost impossible. He couldn't believe that they'd come up so quickly. Earlier in the day, he and his wife, Jill, had been sitting on the grass in Golden Square enjoying the sunshine and he'd kicked off his sandals as he wandered around. Within two hours of their return home the first of the blisters had appeared and now, with the time approaching 10.46 p.m., the pain seemed to be intensifying. He wondered if he'd stepped in some dog shit at first but had been relieved to find he hadn't. Even if he had, he wouldn't have expected his feet to swell up like two pounds of unwrapped mince.

There was another blister on his shoulder and a smaller one on his stomach, both of which were throbbing mightily, but David did his best to ignore the pain. He stretched out on the bed, naked, listening to the sounds of running water from across the landing. He closed his eyes and tried to picture his wife beneath the spray of the shower, and as he did, his penis began to stir into life.

They had been married for almost seventeen years. She had been twenty then, three years his senior. During the intervening years Jill had presented him with two daughters, both of them as beautiful as their mother. He never ceased to marvel at how his wife had managed to retain her shape despite the onset of years. Although thirty-seven was by no means old, she worked hard to keep her figure and that hard work certainly paid off as far as David was concerned. They were a rarity in the world of quick divorces and unhappy relationships. They had managed to keep that spark of romance and excitement which even the closest couples eventually lose to some degree. David knew that the time would come sooner or later, but as yet, their love for each other and, more importantly to him, their passion, showed no signs of abating.

Saturday night was something special for them. The girls were packed off to their grandparents and David and Jill had the house to themselves for what they jokingly called 'depravity night'. It was one of the little rituals which made their lives more enjoyable. David knew, at this minute, that his wife was in the bathroom applying her make-up. Another minute or two and she would be with him.

He tried to forget the blisters and also the nagging pain which had settled like a clamp around the base of his skull.

He heard the sound of footsteps crossing the landing and he closed his eyes, aware now that she had entered the room.

'I thought you'd nodded off,' Jill said softly and he opened his eyes and looked at her, his face a combination of pride and longing.

She was wearing a white basque, the red lace across the front pulled tight to accentuate the curve of her waist and the full swell of her breasts. Her long blonde hair cascaded over her shoulders, attractively framing her youthful, sensual face. Her cheeks were rouged and her slightly parted lips were painted a brilliant red.

David felt his penis growing to full erection as she moved closer to the bed and his gaze roved lower, delighting in this vision of sexuality. She walked slowly and gracefully, her long legs encased in fine silk stockings, the red high-heeled ankle-strap shoes she wore making her look even taller. She stood beside the bed for a moment, hands on hips, allowing him a full view of her stunning form, then she raised one leg and placed her foot on the bed beside him. He swung himself around until he was sitting on the edge of the bed facing her, his eyes following her right hand as it moved slowly across her belly then down between her legs. There she used her index finger to open the gash of her crotchless knickers, allowing the digit to brush through her pubic hair. She rotated it gently, arousing herself.

David leant forward but she stopped him, that finger still working feverishly.

'You watch,' she whispered and began using two fingers. He caressed the inside of her thighs, the feel of the slinky material exciting him even more. He could feel her tensing every so often and her breathing was becoming heavier. David reached up and expertly unfastened the lace which secured the basque, working it free until he exposed Jill's breasts. Her nipples were already swollen and, as David flicked his tongue over them, paying careful attention to each in turn, he felt them harden.

Sensing that her husband's excitement was now reaching fever pitch, Jill lowered her leg and slowly knelt between his thighs, trapping his throbbing organ between her breasts. She rubbed it between the firm mounds, bending her head forward every so often to lick at the bulbous, purple glans which was already leaking clear fluid. He groaned with pleasure as the exquisite torment continued for what seemed like an eternity. She would bring him almost to the point of climax and then stop, repeating the action until she felt his already swollen testicles grow even firmer beneath the kneading action of her fingers.

Jill stood up once more, slipping her knickers off as she did so, standing before him again, only this time she allowed him to use his tongue on her, lapping at her distended vaginal lips. She gripped his shoulders, her red-painted nails digging into his flesh.

He winced as one of them almost touched the blister which was forming there but he fought back the cry of pain.

He planted a kiss on her lathered vagina, then leant back, retrieving something from beneath the pillow.

He held the vibrator before her for a second before flicking it on. Jill smiled as he brought the ten-inch cylinder close to her eager cleft, running it over her mound, teasing her clitoris until she felt like screaming her pleasure. He worked the appliance around her slippery valley, finally pushing it an inch or two into the hot wetness. At the same time his mouth fastened around her hardened bud, his tongue flicking over it. He pushed the vibrator further, increasing the speed as he inserted it.

She held him tighter as the feelings between her legs grew in intensity. David eased her down onto the bed beside him, the humming phallus still embedded in her, only now he began to work it in and out, occasionally rubbing the gleaming tip over her clitoris.

Jill bucked her hips up to meet the thrusts, realizing that the warmth which was spreading around her thighs and belly signalled the beginnings of her first orgasm. She sighed with mild disappointment when David withdrew the vibrator, replacing it with his fingers as he manoeuvred the dripping instrument over her mound to her breasts. Her nipples responded just as willingly to this new-found attention, however, and she reached for his penis, rubbing swiftly but gently, wanting the beautiful torment to continue but also needing the release of a climax.

He lifted the vibrator to her lips, switching it off as he did so. She licked at it, tasting her own juices on the mock phallus, aware of his churning fingers deep within her. He rested his thumb on her clitoris and rubber harder, still pushing the vibrator into her mouth, a slight smile on his face as she licked and sucked it as if it had been his own organ.

He pushed harder and Jill gagged as she felt its tip touch the back of her throat.

Her eyes jerked open and she looked at David, trying to shake her head, to tell him to stop. This part of the game was no longer comfortable.

He increased the pressure, clambering onto her as he did so, the weight of his body pinning her down. She felt a sudden twinge of fear as she looked into his blank eyes and her

151

stomach contracted violently as she felt the sleek cylinder being forced deeper into the maw of her throat. He was using all his weight on it now, and Jill tasted blood as the tissue near her nostrils ripped under the assault. Vomit rushed up from her stomach, filling her mouth, causing her to shudder beneath him.

But still David forced the intruding object further down her throat, stretching her lips wide, until there was barely three inches of it left.

She writhed beneath him in a hideous parody of sexual ecstasy, her eyes rolling upward in the sockets. She tried to cry out but only a liquid gurgle issued forth, and finally her frenzied movements slowed. Then stopped completely.

David looked down at her body. The thick stream of yellowish-red fluid which was spilling from her mouth had stained the sheets and a rancid stench filled his nostrils, but he seemed to take no notice. He rolled off and lay on his back beside the corpse. The pain at the base of his skull was now almost unbearable.

The vibrator still protruded obscenely from his dead wife's mouth.

He could hear its low buzzing as it rattled against her teeth.

As he tried to rise he felt a fresh onslaught of pain, both from his head and also from the newest blister which was bulging from the flesh on the small of his back.

The ones on his shoulder and belly were already weeping pus.

That same night in an area less than a mile square, from Piccadilly to Bloomsbury, another twenty-seven people were killed.

Sunday – the 16th

Twenty-seven

It didn't seem like a Sunday morning.

Inside the large room with its maps and plans tacked to the walls, Alan Finch sat tapping his pen against the notepad before him.

He was seated at a large oval table with eight other men. Every one of them had a pitcher of water in front of him, most of which were already half-empty. Despite the air-conditioning in the room, the blazing early-morning sunshine contrived to turn the room into a hothouse. This was hardly surprising as two sides of the office consisted almost entirely of glass. Through the huge transparent walls the river Thames was clearly visible, licking its way through the city like a dirty parched tongue.

Apart from the occasional aeroplane vapour trail the sky was unblemished. The burning orb of the sun hung against a canopy of blue the colour of faded denim.

Smoke from half a dozen cigarettes eddied in the warm air and many of the ashtrays were already full of dog-ends.

George Bennett waved a hand in front of his face, trying to clear away some of the bluish-grey haze which had settled around him like a fog. It was a curious piece of logic which he'd formulated but which seemed to hold true, that smoke always reached a non-smoker no matter where he was in the room. It was probably only his imagination, but Bennett longed for a fan at this precise moment. Anything to clear the air. The pathologist was nibbling on a whole-wheat biscuit, looking impatiently around him.

Finch rubbed one hand across his stubbled cheeks and

wished that he'd had time to shave before arriving at New Scotland Yard but he'd received the call at eight o'clock and they'd told him it was urgent. He hadn't slept too well the previous night, his mind occupied with thoughts of Theresa and Chris. Would she follow his advice and leave London, he wondered? He could only pray that she would.

He cast quick appraising glances at the other men seated around the table and found that, apart from Bennett, he recognized only Detective Inspector Grogan and DS Nicholson. It had been Bennett who'd called him earlier that morning, asking for his presence at the meeting, though what its purpose was he still didn't know. The pathologist had told him about the incident with the slugs in the sewer the day before and the deaths of the maintenance men. That had been shock enough for Finch but, when he heard that more people had been murdered by victims of the hideous plague and that the crazed killers too had finally succumbed to the monstrous disease, he found his thoughts turning with even more insistence towards his ex-wife and his son. But he also found room in his troubled contemplations for Lisa Foster. He determined to get in touch with her and, if she hadn't already done so, urge her too to leave the capital.

His thoughts were interrupted by the tall, grey-haired man in the dark blue uniform who rose to his feet at the far end of the table.

Sir James Hughes was in his early fifties, a slightly built but nevertheless imposing figure. He had been Metropolitan Police Commissioner for the past eight years. His face was pockmarked, deeply pitted around the cheeks, and a nasty crescent-shaped scar curved from one corner of his mouth giving him the appearance of having a perpetual sneer. He coughed loudly and tapped the table.

'If we could get down to business, gentlemen,' he said, his voice low and rasping as if his throat were full of gravel.

All eyes turned in his direction and a relative hush replaced the muted babble of conversation of a moment before.

Hughes turned to face a large map of Central London which was fastened to a cork board. He stood before it for a moment, as if lost in his own private thoughts, then he jabbed a finger at the Soho area.

'If we take this as the hub of the wheel,' he began, 'for at least half a mile in all directions incidents were reported last night and there have been others over the past week.' He exhaled deeply. 'Now, I just about managed to believe that there was some kind of virus or disease in the city simply because there had been so many similar cases reported. What I did find hard to believe and, if it wasn't for so much evidence, I still wouldn't believe, is the presence of these ... slugs in the sewers.'

'Surely the disease is the first priority to be dealt with,' said Bryant, an official from the Department of Health. He was dressed in a checked jacket, immaculately clean, and as he spoke he pulled at one end of a well-groomed moustache.

'The disease is *caused* by the slugs,' Bennett interrupted. 'The two problems are not independent of one another.'

'Do you honestly believe that there are flesh-eating slugs in the sewers of London?' the man with the moustache said, barely hiding a smile.

'I lost three of my men to the bloody things yesterday,' Donald Robertson barked.

'There is no disputing that the slugs exist and that their ... feeding habits are as we feared,' Hughes said. 'The question is, how do we deal with the problem.' He looked at Bennett. 'Or should I say problems?'

'Why can't we just destroy them?' asked Bryant, tugging at his moustache again.

'I wish it were as easy as that, Mr Bryant,' Hughes said. 'There are reckoned to be hundreds of thousands of them by this time.'

'Well, how the hell did they get down there in the first place?' Bryant grunted indignantly.

'If we knew that, we wouldn't have this problem, would we?' snapped Robertson.

'That's not strictly true,' Finch interjected. 'Even if someone had known where these slugs came from, and how they got into the sewers, no one could have stopped them from multiplying. The sewers are a perfect breeding ground and they also make it easy for them to move around.'

Hughes picked up a manila file folder from the table and flipped it open.

'Mr Dowd.' He looked at the other Water Board official. 'Your report says that the slugs are blocking a number of filters in the sewer tunnels. That's what is causing the overflows of effluent into the streets and homes in these areas.' He hooked a thumb over his shoulder at the map.

Dowd nodded.

'But there's no way of clearing the filters,' he said. 'There are too many slugs.'

'So, in other words, anyone living in the affected area will have to contend with raw sewage pumping out of their drains for as long as the slugs are down there?' Bob Archer said, irritably.

Archer was a year or two younger than Bryant, a lean-faced individual with darting blue eyes. He had been with the Department of Health for over five years, but had never been confronted with a problem of this magnitude before.

'Do you want *your* men to try unblocking the filters?' Robertson snapped at him, challengingly.

Hughes raised a hand for silence, fully aware of the strain which everyone in the room was under. Not least himself.

'We do have one option,' he said, slowly. 'Perhaps the only one.'

The others looked at him expectantly.

'We can evacuate people from the affected area.'

There was a moment's silence, broken by Grogan. The DI lit another cigarette and drew on it.

'We haven't got the men to supervise an operation as big as that, sir,' he said.

'I realize that, Grogan,' Hughes told him. 'We'd need help. From the army. It's the only way I can see of avoiding further deaths.' He shrugged. 'Clear the entire area.'

'But that doesn't take care of the slugs,' said Bennett.

'Or the disease,' Finch added.

'We don't know how far they've spread through those

tunnels,' the pathologist continued. 'If we evacuate one area of the city then they'll simply move on to another area where the food supply is more plentiful.'

'And we can't clear the entire city, sir,' Grogan said.

'Well, at the moment, evacuating at least the critical area seems the best and *only* choice we have,' the commissioner insisted. 'The question is, how to begin.'

'What about broadcasting a warning over the TV and radio?' Archer suggested.

'No,' Hughes said flatly. 'That would cause a panic. We've got enough to contend with without people fleeing in their thousands from the city, clogging the roads and getting in each other's way. We'd have more deaths from road accidents than we would from the slugs or their disease.'

'I wouldn't bet on it,' Bennett commented cryptically.

'Well, I agree with the commissioner,' said Bryant. 'Evacuation seems to be the only solution.'

'The final solution,' murmured Finch, raising his eyebrows when Bennett looked at him. The doctor shrugged, almost apologetically.

'Will you call in the army then, sir?' Grogan asked.

'I'll have to speak to the Home Secretary first,' Hughes told him.

'And in the meantime?' Robertson wanted to know. 'The people in the affected areas are still at risk.'

'They should be warned,' Dowd echoed.

'I told you, I don't want a panic on my hands,' the commissioner snapped.

'You've already got one,' Finch protested in exasperation.

There was a heavy silence as the men looked at their empty notepads as if wanting to avoid eye contact with each other. Every one of them scanned the blank sheets as if they expected some miracle solution to appear magically on them. DS Nicholson was the only one who had used his paper. He'd drawn a cat on it. He looked at the comic sketch, then balled it up, feeling as helpless as the others in the room.

'The area must be sealed off and evacuated,' Hughes repeated. 'It's the only way. The army will have to assist.'

'What makes you think they're any better prepared for this than your own men, or anyone else for that matter?' Robertson said, chewing his nails.

'Have you got any better suggestions?' the commissioner snapped.

'So, assuming all the people can be cleared from the affected areas,' Bennett said, slowly, 'I repeat, what do you intend to do about the slugs?'

'I was hoping that you might have some answers on that score. You and the doctor,' Hughes said. 'You are supposed to be men of science. How would you suggest we kill them?'

'Salt kills slugs, doesn't it?' said Bryant, smiling. 'Let's just hope they decide to attack a Saxa factory.' He chuckled.

Bennett shot him an acid glance and the Health Officer coloured beneath the pathologist's glare.

'Have you *any* ideas?' Hughes said, hopefully.

'Poison of some kind,' Finch suggested. 'But there's no guarantee it would work.'

'What kind of poison?' Grogan asked.

Finch shrugged.

'Something non-combustible if possible,' he said. 'With the amount of methane in those tunnels any explosion down there would bring half of London down with it.'

'Cyanide,' Bennett offered. 'It would be absorbed on contact. It's a fast worker.'

'Have you any idea how many gallons would be needed to flood those tunnels?' said Robertson. 'And besides, where the hell do you think it would go afterwards? All effluent is eventually re-cycled into drinking water and you're talking about using cyanide in it.'

'Also,' Edward Dowd added, 'if the filters are blocked, which we know they are, the cyanide would bubble up into the streets.'

'All the more reason to evacuate those areas then,' the Commissioner said with an air of finality.

'If we can't use poison,' Grogan said, 'what the hell do we do? Go down there and shoot the fucking things one at a time?' He shrugged and swallowed hard, angry with himself for swearing.

'What we all seem to be forgetting is those people infected by the disease,' Robertson said. 'If it turns them into raving maniacs like you said, then the army is going to have its hands full coping with them.'

'The disease works very quickly on the nervous system,' Finch said. 'It has a very short incubation period, perhaps six hours. After that, the victim is lucky to survive much longer than two hours, depending on the severity of the infection.'

'Two hours is plenty long enough to kill somebody,' said Grogan, crushing out his cigarette in the ashtray.

Commissioner Hughes drew a hand across his forehead and sighed.

'I don't think there's anything more we can do at the moment,' he said. 'I'll contact the Home Secretary immediately and get clearance. We'll start the evacuation as soon as possible.'

'And what about the people *not* being evacuated?' said Bennett. 'What do we tell them? That they'd better move just in case they're next on the bloody menu?' His voice carried a note of scorn.

Hughes ignored the question.

'We'll see what the army can do,' he said. Then, turning to Grogan, 'You and your men are to give them every support.' He paused for a moment, licking his dry lips. 'Grogan. Some of the people in the affected areas are likely to be homicidal, psychotic. See to it that at least three men in each unit are issued with sidearms.'

The words hung in the air, like the wreaths of cigarette smoke.

'Anyone dangerous, anyone infected is to be shot.'

Twenty-eight

As he and the other men left the room, Finch felt an almost crushing weariness descend upon him. While Bryant, Archer, Robertson and Dowd all hurriedly left the building, Grogan and Nicholson remained in the commissioner's office. The doctor himself, with Bennett, wandered across the corridor to the washrooms opposite.

While Bennett relieved himself, Finch filled a sink with cold water and splashed his face.

'Shoot on sight,' said Bennett, contemplatively. 'You know, that might have even sounded funny if Hughes hadn't meant it.'

'It's a bit drastic, isn't it?' Finch said, cupping more water in his hands and dousing his face. He blinked hard, as if trying to waken himself.

'What choice do they have?'

Finch studied his reflection in the mirror above the sink. His face looked pale, his eyes were red-rimmed, the whites criss-crossed by veins which stood out prominently. He wouldn't have thought it possible but he looked as rough as he felt.

'Could one of the infected victims be cured?' he pondered aloud.

'Only time will tell, my friend,' Bennett said, zipping up his flies and crossing to the other wash basin. 'But time is one thing we don't have.'

There was a moment's silence, then Finch looked at the pathologist.

'Are you married?' he wanted to know.

162

Bennett smiled and nodded.

'For almost twenty years.'

'Any children?'

'No.' His voice took on a note of sadness. 'We had a daughter but she died when she was eight. Some stupid bastard hit her with his car. The police never did find him.' He swallowed hard, then attempted a casual shrug, attempting to dismiss the memories.

'You never had any more children, then?' Finch said.

'We couldn't bear to risk that kind of pain again. Anyway, why the sudden interest in *my* domestic life?' He smiled.

'I was just curious.'

'Curiosity. The prerogative of doctors and pathologists. Quite an apt quote, don't you think?'

'Who said it?'

Bennett chuckled.

'I did, I just made it up.'

Finch let the water out of the bowl and dried his hands and face on the nearby towel-roll. Then he headed for the door.

'Where are you going?' Bennett wanted to know.

'I'll see you later,' was the doctor's only answer. Bennett found himself alone in the washroom.

Finch found two public phones on the ground floor, close to the main entrance of the building. He ducked inside the plastic canopy of the nearest one and fumbled in his trouser pocket for change. He dialled the number, then waited for what seemed like an eternity until the receiver was picked up at the other end. As the rapid pips sounded in his ear he pushed in some coins.

'Hello,' he said, one part of his mind wishing that the phone hadn't been answered.

There was a crackle of static then he heard an all-too-familiar voice.

'Hello. Who's calling?' Richard Crane asked.

Finch gripped the receiver until it seemed that it would break.

'Hello,' Crane repeated.

If Crane was still at the house, then so too were Chris and Theresa, Finch thought almost angrily. He glared at the receiver, hearing the other man's voice becoming more agitated.

'If this is someone playing silly buggers...' rasped Crane.

Finch knew that all he had to do was ask if his ex-wife and his son were there. Perhaps they *had* left without Crane.

'For the last time,' Crane snarled.

Ask if Theresa and Chris are there.

'OK, pal, have it your own way. Fuck you.'

There was a muted crack as the receiver was slammed down at the other end and Finch was left listening to the slow buzz of the dial tone. He dropped the phone gently back onto its cradle, then turned and headed for the main doors.

The sun was only an hour from reaching its zenith and the tarmac felt hot beneath the soles of his shoes as he walked across the car park, trying to locate his Chevette. The fact that it was a Sunday made no difference in the number of vehicles present. Marked and unmarked cars stretched away in profusion on either side of him. Just another working day. Criminals didn't take weekend breaks, thought Finch as he found his own car. The metal of the door handle was uncomfortably hot. He slid behind the wheel, immediately winding down both front windows in an effort to drive out some of the sickly, cloying heat.

As he pulled away he felt a slight breeze on his face. Even that was warm. Perspiration beaded on his face, but despite the unbearable temperatures Finch felt a peculiar coldness within himself.

He looked at his watch and saw that it was 11.36 a.m.

He swung the car in the direction of Kensington, hoping that the drive would not be too tortuous.

Twice during the journey he almost hit, or was hit by, another car. It was as if his concentration had evaporated as surely as rain beneath the scorching sun. Finch gripped the wheel tighter, trying to focus his mind on his driving. Visions of Chris and Theresa kept surfacing to torment him.

Perhaps he was a little disturbed by the depth of feeling which he found he still had for her. Despite their abrasive meetings he retained an affection for her which he sometimes wished he could discard. But at the moment all he could think of was the safety of his family.

He prayed that for once she had listened to reason and left the city as he'd asked, but as he turned the car into Melbury Road, he felt that icy coldness gripping him once more.

Finch parked the car two or three houses away and walked back. The street was relatively quiet apart from an elderly couple who were out for their pre-lunch stroll, and further down, a young lad who was busy cleaning his car. The doctor thought how peaceful everything looked.

It was hard to imagine that just a mile away, around Soho, Piccadilly and Bloomsbury, the streets were running with sewage and the police were probably already starting to move in to begin the evacuation operation.

Finch walked up the path to the front door and knocked three times.

There was no answer.

He tried again.

Still nothing.

Had they left between the time of his call and his arrival here? He hoped so.

He looked around but could see no sign of the car which Theresa drove. The red Renault which he'd bought her shortly after they'd married was nowhere to be seen. He'd knock once more, he decided, then leave.

He was about to turn away from the door when he heard sounds of movement inside and his heart sank.

Richard Crane opened the door, his face immediately darkening when he saw Finch.

'What the hell do you want?' Crane snapped.

'I want to see Theresa and Chris,' the doctor told him.

Crane snorted.

'Do you?' he rasped.

'If Theresa told you to send me away...'

Crane cut him short.

'She's not here,' he snarled. 'She left about two hours ago, took Christopher with her.'

'Where did she go?'

'She didn't say. All she did say was that *you'd* told her Christopher could be in danger if they stayed in London. Now I want to know what the fuck you've been telling her. I tried to get her to stay but she wouldn't listen to me.'

'Be thankful she didn't Richard,' Finch said calmly. 'Why didn't you go with her?'

'Leave the city because you think there's some disease wiping out the population? What do you take me for? You've always disliked me, haven't you? Because I took what was yours.' His voice was thick with sarcasm. 'Well, I *didn't* take her, she left because she'd had enough of you, but you couldn't let it rest, could you? Sticking your fucking nose in where it's not wanted and now, because of you, she's left.'

'I was thinking of her safety, and Christopher's. If you had any sense you'd have gone with her.'

'Well why don't *you* go now?' he snarled. 'Fuck off, and if I ever see you back here again I'll flatten you.' Crane slammed the door with an almighty crash that threatened to tear the whole jamb from the wall. Finch walked unhurriedly back towards his car, feeling too greatly relieved to be angry at Crane's behaviour.

At least his son had escaped the nightmare which looked like engulfing the whole of London.

As he started his engine a thought passed briefly through his mind.

He wondered if he would ever see Theresa or Chris again. The thought stayed with him, spinning around inside his head.

Finch drove off purposefully, knowing that there was somewhere else he had to go without delay.

As he stood waiting for the door to be opened, Finch looked around and shook his head. Flaxman Court, or at any rate the road on which the block of flats stood, was awash with reeking brown water, some of which had coagulated. There was a thick, glutinous film of scum over most of the water, and the buzzing of thousands of flies was like the low hum of an invisible generator. The insects landed gleefully on the foul-smelling muck, blissfully oblivious of the nauseating stench rising from it.

The doctor had driven along other streets in a similar condition on his journey from Kensington, some of them so badly flooded that they'd already been sealed off by the Health or Water authorities. The consequent detours had added precious time to his drive but now he stood before the door of the flat, waiting.

Lisa Foster smiled broadly when she opened the door and saw the doctor standing there.

He returned the gesture as best he could but there was no warmth in it.

'Alan, how are you?' she asked, motioning him inside.

'I should be asking *you* that question,' he said, accepting the invitation. They passed through to the sitting room.

'I'm OK now,' Lisa told him. 'I know I did everything for my mother that I could while she was alive. My conscience doesn't trouble me. I cried a lot at first, I still do sometimes, but I feel as if I'm coming to terms with her death. I just wish that it could have helped others in some way. Have there been other incidents of the disease?'

'That's what I'm here about,' he told her. 'I want to ask you a question, well, a favour more than that. Will you leave London? Now. Just pack what you need and go.'

'Is it something to do with the disease?' she said.

'It's spreading, Lisa, and no one can stop it.'

'What about a cure?'

Finch sighed.

'It's the manner in which it spreads that makes it impossible to treat.' He went on to tell her about the slugs, the cysts, the breeding and self-generation.

She listened to it all in silence, the colour slowly draining from her cheeks.

'The slugs are using human beings as food and also as . . . incubators for their eggs,' Finch said in conclusion.

'Then it was slugs that caused my mother's death?' Lisa asked, although it sounded more like an affirmation of the truth.

'The sewage in the streets is going to cause other health problems too,' he told her.

She seemed not to hear his last statement.

'Slugs. It doesn't seem possible.'

'I wish it weren't,' Finch said wearily.

A troubled silence descended, broken by the doctor.

'You didn't answer my question, Lisa. Will you leave London? Please. The army is being called in to evacuate this area anyway . . .' The words trailed off as she shook her head.

'Where am I going to go?' she asked him.

'It doesn't matter. Just leave the city. Go to one of your brothers or sisters. It's not important where you go but you have to get out.'

'Will the whole of the city be evacuated?' she wanted to know.

He shook his head.

'It's difficult to say. That isn't the plan at the moment but no one knows how events will turn out. If the slugs can't be contained in this one area then mass evacuation is the only answer.'

'You said you couldn't cure the people who catch the disease. What will happen to them?'

'The police and army have orders to shoot anyone infected.'

'Fight violence *with* violence,' she said, with obvious disapproval.

'Lisa, for God's sake, this isn't the time to be discussing the morality of the situation. People are going to die, hundreds of them, maybe even thousands, if something isn't done to stop the slugs and those they infect.' He turned away from her, lowering his voice slightly. 'I feel so helpless.' Finch laughed humourlessly. 'I'm supposed to be a doctor but I can't do a damn thing to help anyone. I couldn't even help your mother, or that young lad who was brought to me.'

'You can't blame yourself, Alan,' Lisa told him.

168

He turned to face her again.

'I may not be able to cure those who are already infected but at least I can try to stop some people from being killed. That's why I came here, to ask you to leave London before it's too late.'

'I haven't got anyone left now my mother's dead. The rest of my family are like strangers to me. I'm like you, Alan. We're both alone. Let me stay with you, let me help. I owe it to my mother.'

Finch shook his head almost imperceptibly, his gaze lowered. But he didn't speak.

'You're staying even though you say you can't do anything to help the victims,' Lisa continued. 'You're staying because you owe it to yourself, to your own pride. That's the reason *I* won't leave. I watched my mother die, Alan, I'm not running out now. Not when I know that others are suffering like she did.'

Finally he looked at her, seeing and hearing a strength which before he had only glimpsed. Now that strength, that fire, was on full view. During his career, Finch had learned that different people reacted to death in different ways. Lisa was showing it a defiant face, daring it to meet her head-on as it had met her mother.

He nodded, a slight smile on his lips.

'Come on,' he said, quietly. 'We've got to go. You'd better get some clothes together.'

Lisa rose and hurried off to her bedroom while Finch crossed to the sitting room window and looked out at the scum-splashed street.

An army landrover had come to a halt opposite, and as he watched, four men, automatic rifles held across their chests, jumped down from the back of the vehicle and split up, each of them making for a different door.

'Ready,' Lisa called, emerging from the bedroom with a large black hold-all. Finch turned to look at her and smiled his approval. She had changed into a pair of jeans, faded blue tennis shoes and a white T-shirt. Finch took the bag from her and they left the flat, walking close together, passing one of the soldiers as they approached the doctor's car.

As he pulled away, Finch glanced across at his companion, who was busy fastening her long brown hair into a pony tail. She suddenly didn't look so vulnerable anymore. Her face, though still delicately feminine, was now set in hard lines which mirrored the determination within her.

He drove on.

Twenty-nine

Despite Sir James Hughes' insistence that the evacuation of the affected areas should be completed with as little fuss as possible, by 3.59 that Sunday afternoon television news-flashes on both the BBC and ITV networks had informed most of the country of what was happening in Soho, Bloomsbury and Piccadilly.

Those who didn't see the news on TV heard it on the radio, or by word of mouth.

The following day they would read about it in their papers. Some newspapers would even report that London was facing a plague almost on a par with 1665.

As yet, the tide of fear was rising quickly but quietly.

By morning it would have reached panic level.

Telephone switchboards were jammed as relatives and friends outside London tried to contact those in the city.

The police arrested at least a dozen people for looting evacuated houses.

Over fifty bodies were discovered in and around the area dubbed somewhat dramatically 'The Danger Zone'. Of those found, at least half had died of the disease. Most of the others had been their unfortunate victims.

A man was found with a carving knife embedded in his eye – its final resting place after his wife had used it to stab him approximately thirty-four times. She was lying in another room, dead of the contagion.

A woman and her child were found dismembered, but their killer, at the time, was nowhere to be found. He was later seen running down an alley, attempting to bury the axe he carried in the back of a policeman.

A corporal in the Coldstream Guards shot the man dead.

Four of the bodies discovered had been devoured by slugs.

The police and army had been given orders that only specially-equipped units were to remove the bodies of the dead. This they did with the utmost care, placing the corpses in transit vans so that they could be transported to the goods yard at Euston. Here massive funeral pyres had been built and the corpses were immolated under the watchful eye of members of the army medical corps.

When this particular piece of news reached the press there was a great deal of protest from the public.

The Prime Minister appeared on television that evening to assure the viewers that the situation was *under control*, the Whitehall euphemism for 'we couldn't give a fuck as long as it doesn't affect us'.

And, as yet, it didn't.

Despite the catalogue of horrors which escalated gradually through Sunday and into Monday, the deaths, the slug attacks and the disease did, indeed, remain where they had originated.

But how long this state of affairs would last no one knew.

The evacuation continued.

The house searches continued.

More bodies were found.

By 1.06 a.m. on Monday, the police and the army had effectively sealed off the 'Danger Zone'.

Deep below ground the slugs waited.

Monday – the 17th

Thirty

He hadn't slept very well the previous night, but Alan Finch still felt almost abnormally alert. His mind was so crammed with thoughts and ideas that he had found it almost impossible to rest. He could remember dozing for a couple of hours, but after the phone had rung at about six that morning he hadn't bothered settling back for another hour. He'd jumped out of bed, taken a long shower and dressed. At half past six he'd wandered downstairs and made coffee and toast. He'd sat at the kitchen table watching the breakfast TV news on the little black and white portable on the worktop as he sipped the hot black coffee.

The evacuation of dwellings in and around Bloomsbury, Piccadilly and Soho was progressing well but there were still a great many people to be moved. Many, of course, had left of their own accord after hearing what was happening from the media, but the task was by no means complete even if it was, as the newsreader put it, 'well in hand'.

The phone call which had roused Finch from his light slumber had been from the police, telling him that his surgery could not be used again until further notice because it came within the evacuation area. Finch and his colleagues and patients were to use alternative premises near Brompton Road.

The doctor finished his coffee, then got to his feet and headed for the stairs, pausing before the door of the spare room. He knocked lightly and pushed it open, peering around the white-painted partition.

Lisa was still sleeping. She lay on her back, one leg drawn

175

up slightly, the covers pushed back from her naked body.

Finch could not resist a swift glance at her supple form, but then, administering himself a swift mental rebuke, he backed out of the room. He was surprised to find that his cheeks were burning. He managed a faint smile. Was he actually embarrassed? He'd examined dozens of women in his professional capacity. He'd seen more naked bodies than most but not, he told himself, displayed in quite such a provocative fashion as now. He rubbed a hand across his face, then banged on the door loudly, coughing exaggeratedly.

'Lisa,' he called.

'Yes, OK, come in,' she murmured, her voice thick with sleep.

He waited a second, then popped his head around the door once again.

She was sitting up in bed, the sheets pulled above her breasts, her eyes heavy-lidded. He smiled at her and she smiled back sleepily.

'There's toast and coffee downstairs,' he told her.

She thanked him, asked him if she could take a shower and said she'd be down in fifteen minutes. Finch retreated from the room for the second time and returned to the kitchen, where he spooned instant coffee into another mug and replaced the kettle on the stove. As he waited for it to boil he thought about his conversation with Lisa the previous night. She had, it appeared, more or less come to terms with the death of her mother and had spoken freely about her feelings. Finch had listened with interest, his respect growing by the minute for this young woman, who when he'd first seen her less than a week ago had looked so frail and vulnerable.

Less than a week, he thought. Had all this happened so fast? So much pain and suffering in such a short time? It didn't seem possible.

Lisa entered the kitchen a moment later, dressed in the same faded blue tennis shoes but a clean pair of jeans and a sweatshirt. She sat down opposite him and sipped at her coffee. He asked if she'd slept well. She asked him what was going on with respect to the crisis.

Finch repeated what he'd heard on the news.

'One square mile doesn't sound like a very large area,' he continued. 'But there must be hundreds of people who are still in danger, and if the police and army are searching every building individually, there's no wonder it's taking time.'

'Do you think the disease will spread, Alan?' she asked him.

Finch shrugged.

'As long as the slugs continue to breed then I can't see any way of stopping it,' he told her.

'Isn't anyone working on a cure?' she wanted to know.

'There *is* no cure. Once initial contact has been made the incubation period is so short there simply isn't enough time to help the victim. I'm surprised your mother lasted so long...' He stopped in mid-sentence, lowering his gaze. 'Oh, God, I'm sorry, Lisa. I didn't mean to say that.'

She reached across the table and gently touched his hand, holding it until he faced her once more.

'I'm sorry,' he repeated. 'If I'd have been any kind of doctor she probably wouldn't have died.'

'There was nothing more you could have done,' Lisa said. 'Nothing *anyone* could have done would have saved her.'

Finch was about to say something else when there was a loud banging on his front door.

He looked up in surprise, then got to his feet and passed through the sitting room to the hall.

The banging continued until he opened the door.

A uniformed constable stood there.

'Doctor Alan Finch?' he said.

Finch nodded.

'Would you come with me please, sir?' the policeman said, taking a step back, and Finch caught sight of the red-and-white parked closeby. The driver was also looking across at him.

'What's happened?' the doctor wanted to know.

'We were told to pick you up and take you to the Yard, sir. Mr Bennett asked for you to be there. It's important.'

Finch nodded and reached for his coat, turning to see Lisa standing behind him.

'Is something wrong, Alan?' she said, seeing the policeman.

'Come on,' he said. 'You're coming with me.'

'I wasn't told about the young lady, sir,' the constable said. 'I'm not leaving her here alone.'

The uniformed man looked at Lisa, then at Finch. He nodded and headed back to the car, followed by his two charges. They all climbed into the car which, seconds later, sped off.

Thirty-one

Fuck the newspapers. Fuck the TV too, thought Keith Turner as he stood outside the Love Shop gazing at the full length, life size photograph of a naked Chinese girl with long black hair which reached her bottom. Beside this photo was another, similar one of a white girl. Both of the shots were old now, crinkled and yellowing at the edges, but the smiles of the girls as they looked back over their bare shoulders still seemed fresh and inviting to Keith.

Fuck the newspapers, he thought again, fumbling in his trouser pocket for his wallet. He didn't give a shit about any plague or whatever the hell it was they were on about. He'd been coming to the Love Shop every day for the last eight months. No matter which shift he'd worked he always found time to come and see his girls. He felt that they *were* his, he saw more of them than most men. A lot more, he thought with a chuckle. The neon sign over the door was lighted, even though it was only ten o'clock in the morning. Some of the small bulbs in the glowing sign had burned out, but he didn't need to read what it said, he knew it by heart:

Then, below that, in much smaller letters, scrawled with a felt-tip pen on a piece of cardboard and stuck on the door with Blu-Tack:

NO ONE UNDER THE AGE OF 18 ALLOWED PAST THIS POINT.
ANYONE LIKELY TO BE OFFENDED SHOULD NOT ENTER THESE PREMISES.

He pushed open the door and walked in. An unshaded light bulb hung above him, lighting his way as he descended the narrow staircase towards a curtain of beads which hung across the doorway at the bottom. He brushed through it, the beads rattling. There was a small desk immediately to his right. Behind it sat a fat, bearded man in his thirties. He was reading a newspaper and eating fish and chips, wiping his fingers on a dirty T-shirt which bore the slogan:

AIDS TURNS FRUITS INTO VEGETABLES

The smell of the food mingled with a powerful odour of damp but it was one which Keith had come to tolerate, almost welcome. He paid his money to the man, who handed back the change without looking up, his attention still on the paper.

'Any booth,' he said, motioning towards the line of closed doors which confronted Keith.

He walked to the first booth, stepped inside and locked it behind him. The cubicle was no larger than one in a public lavatory. The walls were painted white, or what had once been white. Now they were cracked and peeling, pieces flaking off like scabrous skin. There was a single plastic seat facing what looked like a letterbox. The room smelt musky. The smell of dried perspiration and semen.

Keith seated himself and fumbled in his jacket for the coins he'd brought. There were ten fifty-pence pieces. Enough to give him at least ten minutes' viewing of the girl who, at this moment, waited behind the wall he faced. He liked it early in the morning for, more often than not, he was the only punter in the place. Others didn't start arriving until midday. Before he inserted the first 50p in the appointed slot, Keith unzipped his trousers and freed his penis which was already beginning to swell with anticipation. Smiling, he pushed in the coin and the partition rose, giving him a clear view of the area beyond.

It was about eight feet square, and he could see other peepholes for the booths on the far side. All, at the moment, closed.

There was a girl sitting naked in the middle of the tiny arena smoking a cigarette and chewing on a bacon sandwich. She looked around almost in surprise as the box opened and she found herself the subject of Keith's lecherous gaze. She took a last drag on her cigarette, then stubbed it out and pushed away the sandwich. Vicki hadn't expected any punters as early as this, in fact she hadn't expected any at all after what she'd read in the papers. Standing as it did in Lexington Street, not that far from Soho, she had expected 'Loveshop' to be closed. In fact she had even contemplated not coming to work, but she needed the money. Her kids had to be clothed and fed.

She was twenty-five, two years younger than Keith, but her face was pale and drawn and beneath the harsh lights she looked ten years older. However, almost immediately, the lights dimmed and a thunderous explosion of music filled the place. Vicki got to her feet and began dancing as provocatively as was possible at ten o'clock in the morning with her greasy breakfast slopping around inside her. She moved closer to the peep-hole through which Keith stared, rubbing her hands over her breasts, teasing her nipples in a vain attempt to make them stick out.

Keith began masturbating.

After a minute he swiftly pushed another coin into the slot as the partition began to descend, his other hand speeding up its action on his swollen organ.

Vicki continued her practised gyrations, turning away briefly when she couldn't suppress a yawn.

Keith, his ears filled with the deafening sound of the music, his eyes glued to Vicki, continued rubbing his penis, hoping that he would come before his fifty-pence pieces ran out.

Neither of them heard the screams from outside the booth.

The yells of agony uttered by the fat man as he struggled to escape the black slugs which were feeding on his ample body.

As the partition began to drop once more, Keith shoved in another coin, his breath coming in short gasps now as he watched Vicki's frenzied movements. She licked her lips, then tried to push her large breasts towards her own mouth, flicking at her nipples with her tongue. Christ, she thought, wasn't this bastard ever going to run out of money?

The music pounded away incessantly, covering the soft slurping noises made by the slugs as they eased their way effortlessly beneath the door of the booth. A black trail of them, like spilled oil, flowed from the lavatory of the club, then formed two prongs. One had engulfed the fat doorman, the other was forcing its way inside the small cubicle, like a thin finger trying to prise a path between two narrow surfaces. Even the larger slugs gained access without too much trouble.

Keith saw that he was down to just two coins so he speeded up the movement of his hand, the glorious feelings of orgasm beginning to envelop him.

He stood up, stooping slightly so that he could still see through the slit, but also wanting Vicki to see him.

She realized that he was nearly finished so, as a special treat, she moved closer to the opening, pushing her breasts towards it, allowing Keith to touch the quivering mounds with his free hand. The contact was sufficient. He grunted loudly as he climaxed, white fluid spouting from his penis in thick gouts, some of which splashed Vicki's breasts. She didn't complain, though. She merely smiled her practised smile and looked in at him, watching as he milked the last drops from his organ.

She saw the slugs gathered behind him in the cubicle.

Vicki backed off, her eyes riveted to the monstrous black horde which was moving closer to Keith. She tried to shout a warning but the music was too loud and, to her horror, she saw that the metal slat was beginning to drop once more. She banged on the wall in a last desperate attempt to alert him and then she was left with the insane vision of a man, trousers around his knees and penis clutched in his hand, about to be engulfed by slugs. What a stupid way to die, she thought.

Inside the booth, Keith screamed as the first of the creatures bit into him. Blood spurted from the wounds and he fell to his knees, trying to reach the door, trying to unlock it, but the slimy mass of slugs prevented him from escaping. As they slithered over him, driving their sickle-like teeth into his flesh, he bellowed his agony. The sickly white walls of the cubicle were sprayed crimson as one of the slugs ate through his carotid artery. Keith fell forward into the seething mass.

There was a door at one end of the small arena close to where Vicki stood and she bolted for it, unconcerned about her nakedness, wanting only to escape this unspeakable horror.

The music pounded away relentlessly as she pulled at the door. The wood was swollen with dampness and it did not open easily.

Perhaps the space underneath had been too narrow for them to slide through. Or perhaps they were content to wait. Whatever the reason, the slugs outside had slithered up on top of each other against the door until they were almost at chest height.

Vicki tugged harder and the door flew open.

She had time for one scream before the ravenous wall of black death collapsed upon her.

The music continued to play, masking the obscene sounds made by the feasting slugs.

The foyer of the Regent Palace Hotel in Piccadilly was like a huge, well-decorated mausoleum. As silent as a crypt. Completely devoid of guests or staff. Five members of the Coldstream Guards had arrived an hour earlier to ensure that no one remained in the building. The manager had assured them that the place was empty but they had to be certain.

It took time, as the hotel was one of Europe's largest. Sergeant Derek Pagett and the manager, Martin Forbes, were still walking the labyrinthine corridors in search of any stray guests or staff. Both carried pass keys which would allow them entrance to any room, in the form of electronic cards which would slip the locking mechanism of the door.

Forbes was on the seventh floor. Pagett, he knew, was one floor above him. Every so often, in the unearthly silence which filled the hotel, he would hear movements from above as the sergeant passed swiftly from room to room.

Perspiration was soaking into Forbes' shirt, not all of it, he realized, the product of the scorching day. He moved quickly along the well-lit corridors, his ears alert for the slightest sound. As he reached each bend he would slow down as if expecting someone, or something, to be waiting for him around the next corner.

He pushed on, flinging open the doors which took him past the central staircase.

There were sounds close by.

Heavy footfalls.

Forbes tried to control his laboured breathing, pressing himself back into a doorway as the loud thumps drew nearer.

Pagett came striding through the door to the stairs, his automatic rifle held across his chest.

'Found anything?' he said.

Forbes shook his head gratefully, relieved that he hadn't.

'I'll go down to the sixth floor,' the sergeant said, and thudded off down the stairs.

Forbes hurried along the corridor towards the lifts, his heart thumping just that little bit faster than normal.

In a room to his left he heard a loud bang.

The manager froze, moving nearer, aware that his hands were shaking.

The sound came again.

Like wood on wood.

He reached for the pass key, inserting it into the electronic lock, pressing the slim card down until the green light above the handle flickered on. He swallowed hard and prepared to enter.

There was another bang, and the sound of breathing.

It was a second or two before he realized that the breathing was his own.

He pushed open the door and looked inside.

One of the guests had left the wardrobe door open and the breeze coming through the window had caused it to slam against the frame.

Forbes sighed, closed the door behind him and moved on.

He reached the lifts, satisfied that the seventh floor was clear. Pagett was checking the one below, so he decided to go down to five. All the lifts were on the ground floor so he jabbed the appropriate button and waited for the car to rise. The numbers lit up as it ascended.

One. Two. Three.

The manager took a handkerchief from his pocket and wiped the film of perspiration from his face.

Four. Five.

The quicker he got out of here the better.

Six.

He glanced behind him, half expecting to see one of the diseased maniacs coming at him with a knife.

The lift arrived.

There was no maniac behind him.

The doors slid open.

He stepped in. Pressing button five, he leant back against the rear wall of the car as it descended, quickly bumping to a halt at the designated floor.

Forbes took a deep breath, as if he were about to immerse his head in water, then he stepped out and hurried along the corridor to his right performing the same routine as he'd done on the other floors. As he walked, his feet thumped out a hollow rhythm on the thin carpet, but above him he could hear Pagett's progress.

The knowledge that the sergeant was also in the building brought a small amount of comfort to Forbes, although he dared not think what else might be skulking in one of the still unchecked rooms.

He turned the corner into another corridor and stopped short.

Someone had either turned out the lights or they had blown.

The corridor was in darkness.

Not the impenetrable blackness of night or of an unlit cellar, but still dark enough to send a shiver down his spine at the thought of passing along it. He clenched his fists and walked on into the gloom, his eyes darting furtively from side to side. He tried to swallow but found that his throat had constricted into a tight knot. His heart thumped against his ribs as if trying to escape the confines of his chest.

The lifts were perhaps fifty yards ahead of him.

It seemed like fifty miles.

As Forbes reached what he guessed was roughly the middle of the corridor, he stopped and listened.

There was no sound. Only the blood rushing through his veins, roaring in his ears.

No sound.

Not even that of Pagett and his heavy boots.

Silence.

Fear suddenly hit him like an invisible fist. He had never felt so alone and afraid in his life. A groan of terror escaped him as he stood motionless. He looked back over his shoulder, then ran, pounding down the darkened corridor in a desperate effort to escape the blackness. It seemed to follow him like a living thing until, finally, he emerged into the light, almost stumbling, his legs trembling.

He couldn't stand this any longer, he decided. To hell with it. Let Pagett search the rest of the building.

He didn't bother using the lift but hurtled down the stairs instead, taking them two at a time, his only concern now to be free of the stifling, threatening confines of the hotel.

As he reached the first floor landing he tripped and went sprawling, rolling over several times before crashing into the wall. The impact knocked the wind from him and he lay still for a moment gasping, but spurred on by his terror, he soon clambered to his feet and hurried down the remaining steps towards the foyer.

The stench struck him first.

Forbes slowed his pace as he reached the foyer, held back by the reeking, nauseating odour. Fighting back the urge to vomit, he felt as if he were going to faint.

At first he thought he was imagining what he saw in the foyer, that the fall he'd taken moments earlier had affected his perception in some way. But no, there was no doubt about it.

The floor of the foyer was moving.

Undulating gently as if someone were blowing air underneath it.

It was a second or two before he realized what he was seeing.

Slugs covered every square inch of the large foyer.

A living black carpet of writhing forms which slithered and oozed in their own thick mucoid secretions. The closest and largest of them were already sliding up onto the steps where Forbes swayed unsteadily.

He tried to back away but his foot slid off the edge of a step, causing him to overbalance.

Arms flailing madly, he pitched forward into the mass of slugs.

Many were crushed beneath him, their bodies bursting like overripe fruit, but hundreds more covered his body in a matter of seconds, all eager to taste his flesh.

He managed one deafening scream before a particularly large slug ate through his windpipe.

Up on the fourth floor Sergeant Pagett heard the scream and came running. Simultaneously, the men who waited outside in the Landrover crashed into the building's foyer, stopping short as they saw the slugs, many of which turned and began slithering towards them.

'Get out!' Pagett bellowed at his men as he neared the bottom of the stairs, and they needed no second warning. The sergeant himself looked down and saw that something lay amongst the slugs gathered around the foot of the staircase. An almost shapeless mass which was covered by the black abominations. He saw blood and, with horror, realized that what was beneath the slimy blanket of death was Forbes. One bloodied hand, two of the fingers already eaten to the bone, rose from the mass as if soliciting help.

Pagett gritted his teeth and backed off, raising the rifle to his shoulder. He drew a bead on the point where he guessed Forbes' head to be and fired twice, the thunderous report of the FN echoing around the hotel foyer. The hand dropped and the slug-covered shape remained still. The sergeant muttered something to himself, then glanced towards the main doors of the building. He might just be able to make it across the undulating black sea of slugs, but one slip and he would end up like Forbes.

The sergeant spun round and headed back up the stairs until he reached the large, frosted-glass window at the first landing. Without hesitation he drove his rifle butt through it, shattering the glass. Moving quickly, he hauled himself up onto the ledge, cutting his hands on several jagged shards in the process.

The drop to the street below was perhaps twelve or fifteen feet. It didn't look like much of a distance, except that he would be landing on concrete.

He glanced back into the foyer at the slugs and did not hesitate any longer.

He jumped.

The impact broke both his ankles, the sound of snapping bone audible in the nearly-deserted street, and Pagett rolled over, his face a mask of pain. In a matter of seconds his men were with him, carrying him back to the waiting landrover, away from the hotel.

Away from the slugs.

Thirty-two

As they were escorted from the police car to the main entrance of New Scotland Yard, Finch wondered if this was what a criminal felt like as he was being taken into custody. Flanked on both sides by uniformed men, the doctor almost felt like pulling a blanket over his head. Had the circumstances been different he might well have found the situation amusing. As it was, he and Lisa walked briskly into the building and followed one of the uniformed men to a lift. It carried them to the fifth floor, where they all stepped out into a long corridor which looked somewhat familiar to Finch.

During the journey the doctor had attempted to discover what was going on but the two policemen seemed to know little more than Finch himself. Either that or they'd been instructed not to divulge any information.

The trio stopped outside a door and the constable knocked, leaving them alone as it was opened.

George Bennett smiled at Finch and beckoned him inside, casting a puzzled glance at Lisa. The doctor made swift introductions, explaining the somewhat tenuous reasons for Lisa's presence.

'I'm sorry to hear about your mother,' said Bennett when the doctor had finished.

Lisa smiled thinly at him and sat down in the proffered chair.

Finch nodded greetings to the other men present. To Sir James Hughes. To DI Grogan and a military man he hadn't seen before.

Dressed in combat fatigues, the soldier was in his thirties, perhaps a year or two older than Finch. On the belt round his waist there was a holster and the doctor could see the butt of an automatic pistol protruding from it. The man had bright blond hair which glinted beneath the fluorescents. When he moved, Finch saw that he dragged his left leg slightly.

The soldier looked strangely incongruous alongside the other occupants of the room, Finch thought. And a little menacing too.

Captain Sean Maconnell returned Finch's nod of greeting, reserving an approving glance for Lisa. Maconnell had been an officer in the Coldstream Guards for four years, having risen from the ranks since first joining back in 1966. He came from a family which was anything but steeped in military tradition. His father had spent most of his National Service time in the glass house, and his grandfather had been shot in 1916 as a conscientious objector. Maconnell loved the army, though, and wondered now how he would survive without it. Even after an IRA sniper's bullet had shattered his left hip six years ago, during a raid on an arms cache in the Falls Road, he had pulled through against all odds. The prospect of getting back into uniform had driven him on. For a time, doctors had thought that the Armalite bullet had succeeded in condemning him to crutches for the rest of his life. Maconnell had refused to accept their prognosis, and after months of pain and numerous operations he had managed to walk once more, albeit with a limp. But he didn't complain and only on odd occasions did it still cause him pain.

'Before we start,' Finch said. 'Could someone tell me what's going on? Why was I called?'

He was looking at Bennett but he didn't care who answered the question.

'The affected area has been cleared,' Hughes answered, scratching the scar on his chin. 'We must destroy the slugs now, before they have a chance to move on.'

'But we still don't know how to destroy them,' Finch said.

'We're sticking with the idea of cyanide,' Bennett informed him.

'But it can't be done because of the risk of poisoning,' said Finch, aghast.

Bennett ignored the doctor's protestations.

'As long as the slugs are spread through the tunnels that idea could never succeed. No matter how much cyanide we pumped down into the sewers we couldn't be sure of killing them all,' Finch added.

'If they could be gathered in one place it might just work,' Bennett said, quietly.

'There must be miles of tunnels under that area,' the doctor exclaimed. 'It's impossible.'

'Nothing is impossible,' countered Maconnell, catching Finch's gaze and holding it.

'What we propose to do is to drive the slugs back along the tunnels,' said the officer. 'The sewers would be sealed off one by one until all these bloody creatures were forced into one spot. Then the cyanide could be released.'

'How do you expect to "drive" them?' Finch asked.

'I'll send some engineers down there with flame throwers. Most animals retreat from fire, don't they?'

'You can't use flame throwers,' Hughes said. 'You'd blow up the entire system. We have to find another way.'

Bennett stroked his chin thoughtfully.

'Why *drive* them?' he said. 'Why not use a lure?'

The others looked at him, their expressions ranging from surprise to bewilderment.

'Let the slugs follow something instead. Lead them to the place where they're to be destroyed, don't drive them.'

'And what do we lead them with?' Grogan asked, taking another drag on his cigarette.

'They feed on human flesh, right?' the pathologist said, his tone calm and measured. 'Give them what they want.'

'My God, you're not serious,' Grogan said, gaping in astonishment. 'You want to sacrifice the lives of innocent men just so they can act as fucking bait?'

'What's a dozen or so lives compared to the number it could save?' Bennett challenged.

'There's no guarantee it would work anyway,' the DI persisted.

'I think there is,' the pathologist told him. 'The secretion left by the leading slugs, the slime trails, seems to act as a stimulant for the others. Much the same as pheromones works for ants. The stronger the secretion, the more likely the slugs are to follow it.' He paused. 'Men injected with that secretion would automatically attract the slugs.'

'But if they were injected, they'd die of the disease anyway,' Finch said.

'Not for at least six hours,' the pathologist countered. 'Six hours to clear the tunnels, that's all the time we'd need.'

'That's murder,' said Grogan. 'You're talking about murdering men in cold blood.'

190

'I'm talking about saving the rest of this city, millions for Christ's sake,' Bennett snapped. 'It's the only way.' He studied the faces of the others in the room. 'Don't look at me passing moral judgements, you all know I'm right.'

Commissioner Hughes turned and looked at the map of the sewer tunnels.

'How would we go about it?' he said, quietly, almost conspiratorially.

'Sir, you can't be serious,' Grogan interrupted.

The commissioner turned on him, eyes blazing.

'What choice do we have?' he snapped. 'I don't like this any more than you. I wish there *was* another way but there isn't.'

The two men regarded each other coldly for a moment then Grogan shook his head resignedly.

'The men would be put into the sewer tunnels ahead of the slugs,' Bennett said. 'They'd move in front of the hordes until they converged at a place where the cyanide could be released.'

'That gives them a great choice,' Grogan snapped. 'They either get eaten alive, poisoned or die of this fucking disease.'

'How would we seal the tunnels?' Maconnell wanted to know.

'Groups of your men could follow the slugs, at a safe distance. The tunnels could be brought down when the signal was given. The men following wouldn't be in danger as long as they kept well back. The slugs would be too intent on following the infected men.'

'So first we pinpoint where the slugs are concentrated,' Hughes said, studying the map again. He lowered his voice slightly. 'God, there must be so many of them.'

'That shouldn't be too difficult,' Maconnell said. 'Find the location of their last victims and they should be in the vicinity.'

'Where are you going to obtain the secretion in order to inject the men?' Finch wanted to know.

'From the slugs that hatched from that young boy's body,' the pathologist told him.

'What do we tell the men who are infected?' Grogan asked. 'That they're going to be used as food for slugs? That if the slugs don't get them they're going to die anyway?'

'We tell them nothing,' Hughes said before the pathologist could answer. He sighed. 'If any of them do make it out of the tunnels, Bennett, what happens to them then? We can't just sit around and watch them die.'

Bennett swallowed hard, then shrugged. When he spoke, his voice was low.

'They'll have to be killed. Shot, if the disease is too far advanced by the time they emerge.'

'Like rabid dogs, eh?' grunted Grogan.

An uneasy silence settled, almost as if the enormity of the proposed solution had robbed the room's occupants of the ability to speak.

Grogan lit another cigarette. Bennett sat with his hands folded on his lap, head lowered slightly.

Finch got up, went over to the map of the sewers and studied it carefully.

'The effluent will be re-cycled into drinking water,' he murmured. 'Remember what the Water Board men told us? We can't use cyanide to kill the slugs.'

'But the area where they'll be destroyed will be sealed off,' Maconnell protested.

'The slugs might not be able to get out but, short of building walls, there's no way we're going to be able to stop that poison reaching these other tunnels.' He ran his finger over the diagram. 'And, eventually, the Thames.'

'It's the only solution we have,' Hughes told him. 'We can't burn them, we can't blow them up. Poison is the only alternative.'

Finch was looking at the diagram again, narrowing his eyes as he studied several other lines, some drawn in blue, which ran parallel with the sewer tunnels.

'What are these?' he asked, indicating the lines.

'They're electricity cables,' Grogan told him.

Finch turned and looked at the others in the room, a slight smile on his face.

'That's how we destroy them,' he said. 'Electrocute them.'

Bennett too found that he could smile. He nodded admiringly.

'Would it work?' Hughes wanted to know.

'I don't see why not,' Bennett told him. 'A large enough current applied for long enough ought to kill them and there's no better conductor than water.'

'What sort of voltage do those cables carry?' Maconnell asked.

'We don't need to use those,' Hughes said. 'We can set up portable generators. When the slugs have been drawn into position we'll fry them.' He chuckled.

Maconnell smiled broadly.

For the first time, Lisa spoke.

'There's one thing you haven't decided,' she said, quietly. 'Who's going to be the bait? Which men go into the sewers?'

Thirty-three

At 10.28 that morning, men of the Royal Engineers succeeded in locating the first mass of slugs. They were between Dean Street and Shaftesbury Avenue in a mid-level tunnel.

Five minutes later a second group were discovered in a storm-relief sewer under Brewer Street.

A wider sweep of the area revealed the third, and largest, concentration of the creatures beneath Sherwood Street.

They appeared to be stationary, but for how long no one dared guess.

The officers in charge of each detachment of engineers relayed the information to Maconnell, who was still at New Scotland Yard, then to units of police who were also in the vicinity of Piccadilly.

Bennett lifted the last slug from the jar and deposited it in a specimen tray normally reserved for human organs. The pathologist watched the writhing black monstrosities for a moment with a mixture of fear and loathing. Some were as much as five inches long, and as thick as his index finger. He carried the tray across the lab and set it down carefully on the other workbench, his eyes never leaving the slugs, which were sliding up the sides. He knocked one back with the sharp end of a scalpel, severing one of its eye-stalks as he did. Then, opening a cupboard above him, the pathologist took out a bottle of sulphuric acid and unscrewed the stopper. He poured the lethal liquid over the slugs, watching almost gleefully as the corrosive fluid ate into their soft, slimy bodies. A choking stench rose to fill his nostrils but he continued to gaze at the creatures. The tray began to fill up with a sickly yellow mixture of pus and slime as the last of the slugs simply dissolved. Bennett emptied the glutinous contents down the sink then ran the hot tap, washing away the last vestiges of corruption. He dropped the tray in a plastic bag and sealed it, knowing that he must dispose of it as soon as possible, then he returned to the jar and peered in.

There was a thick, reeking coagulation of mucus at least two inches deep inside it.

The pathologist took the first of three syringes laid out close to him and drew off some of the slime. He then filled the rest of the receptacle with saline solution so that the fluid would flow more easily in the bloodstreams of the men to be injected.

He paused for a moment, sighing.

The plan to infect men with the disease had been his idea. An honest attempt to solve what was becoming an increasingly insoluble problem. But as he looked at the syringe and its deadly contents, he realized just how close to the truth Grogan had been.

Bennett was condemning at least a dozen men to the most agonising and horrific death imaginable.

He tried to balance that view against his own feeling that the sacrifice was necessary in order to save many more lives, but still that nagging doubt continued to surface in his mind.

Murderer.

The word flashed brightly in his mind's eye like a neon sign.

Think how many would be saved, though?

But the men who are going to die. They have families.

It's a small sacrifice.

Will their wives, girlfriends, children and parents agree with you?

Bennett stood still for a moment, resting his arms on the work top, trying to clear his mind, attempting to stop the endless self-accusations.

This *was* the only way, he told himself, filling another syringe.

As he did so, he noticed that his hands were shaking slightly.

At 10.43 six large Scania lorries arrived in Piccadilly Circus. They parked in a rough semi-circle around the Eros monument.

Detective Inspector Ray Grogan watched as troops and police opened the back doors of the lorries.

Inside each one was a KVA 1000 portable generator, fifteen feet long and as tall as a man. The machines were given a hasty check-over by the civilian engineers who maintained them.

As Grogan looked on, cables were run from the generators to the open manholes and were lowered into the gloom below until they entered the stinking water. The roar of the Scania engines was replaced by a loud hum as the machines were switched on.

They were ready.

Cables as thick as a man's arm criss-crossed Piccadilly, lying there like slumbering snakes, waiting for the power to be pumped through them.

Grogan drew another cigarette out of his rapidly dwindling packet and looked at his watch.

It was 11.04.

At 11.18 one hundred men of the First Battalion, Coldstream Guards, drew lots to decide who would descend into the sewers. They were not told the purpose of the selection. One hundred pieces of paper, twelve of them marked with an 'X', had been folded and placed in a cardboard box.

It took less than five minutes for the dozen marked scraps to be retrieved.

The men holding them were ordered out into a waiting truck, and their companions sent back to their positions around Piccadilly.

The twelve men were driven to New Scotland Yard in the truck, escorted down to the pathology lab and told to wait outside.

'I wish somebody would tell us what the bleeding hell's going on,' said Private Terry Banks, shifting his feet nervously. He scratched his chubby face and looked around at his companions.

'No doubt we just 'volunteered' for something,' Chas Granger told him.

'What kind of thing?' Banks insisted.

'If we knew that we wouldn't be standing around here with our thumbs up our arses wondering, would we?' chided Pat Morrissey.

'Shut it, will you,' snapped Simon Johnson. 'Let's see what the fucking hell they want before we start getting uptight about it.' As he was a corporal, Johnson's voice carried some authority and the men duly stopped talking.

'I wish I'd got a fag,' murmured Banks, chewing the nail of his index finger.

An acid glance from Johnson silenced him.

'Come on, corp,' said Morrissey. 'What do you reckon's going on? Why do they want us?'

'They don't necessarily want *us*,' Johnson said. 'We just happen to be the silly fuckers who drew the wrong lots.'

The men suddenly drew themselves to attention as the door of the lab was opened and they saw Captain Maconnell standing there.

'Stand easy,' he said.

The men did, but they didn't relax.

'Come inside one at a time,' Maconnell said and ushered Granger forward, closing the door behind him.

Banks tried to move to a position further down the line but Johnson shook his head.

'You're next Banks,' he said. 'You wouldn't want to miss the surprise would you?'

The private muttered something under his breath but his audible murmurings were silenced when the lab door opened again. Granger did not emerge but Banks was ordered inside.

As he entered the room he saw his companion sitting on the far side of the lab.

'Roll up your right sleeve,' said Bennett brusquely, careful to avoid looking at Banks too closely, especially at his eyes. These men he was sending to their deaths must, for him, remain faceless. He brandished the hypodermic before him, gripped Banks' wrist and then ran the needle into the pulsing fat vein in the crook of his arm, pressing down carefully on the plunger, forcing 10ml of the lethal fluid into the soldier's bloodstream. Banks winced until the needle was pulled free. Bennett pushed a swab into his free hand and told him to press it against the tiny puncture until it stopped bleeding.

Banks went and sat next to Granger and the two men watched as the same procedure was carried out, with dizzying speed, on their ten companions.

When he'd finished, Bennett washed his hands.

Would guilt wash off?

He looked at Maconnell and the officer nodded, turning towards his men.

'I'm going to keep this as short and simple as I can,' he said. 'No doubt you're all wondering what's happening.' He cleared his throat, as if to make the words come forth more easily. Finally the Captain looked away and banged the work top angrily. 'Fuck it,' he rasped. His face was set in hard lines when he turned back to look at the troops. 'You're going to enter the sewer tunnels,' he said flatly, perhaps reasoning that the lie coming next wouldn't taste so bitter if it were said quickly.

'Two of our men are down there, they've got to be found. You'll be split into three groups, four men in each. Work your way towards Piccadilly, you'll find ladders leading up from the sewer tunnels where you can get out.' He tried to swallow but his throat was as dry as chalk.

'What were the shots for, sir?' Johnson asked.

It had all been rehearsed well and Maconnell did not falter as he answered.

'As you know, the slugs pass on a disease through their slime trails. The shots will protect you against that disease.' The last few words were forced out through clenched teeth. 'Are there any questions?'

'What about the two blokes who are missing, sir?' Banks wanted to know. 'What if they've got this disease? It's incurable, isn't it?'

Maconnell nodded.

'Just find them,' he said, struggling now to retain his composure. He felt like apologizing to the men, telling them the truth. The Captain finally turned away from them. 'There's a truck waiting to take you to the designated entry points. You'll descend into the sewers there.'

The men stood as one and saluted before filing out, the last one closing the lab door behind him.

As the sound of their footsteps receded down the corridor Maconnell faced the pathologist.

'There was no other choice,' Bennett said. 'Don't you think I would have found another answer if I could?'

'Damn you, Bennett, those are my men,' hissed the Captain. 'They trust me and I've just given them a bullshit story, knowing that I'm sending them to their deaths.'

'Don't think you've got the monopoly on conscience, Maconnell,' the pathologist said, quietly.

The Captain headed for the door, pausing briefly as he reached it. 'Damn you anyway,' he snarled. 'Damn you for being right.' The door slammed and Maconnell was gone.

Bennett stood alone, the only sound in the lab the slow, steady ticking of the wall clock. He glanced at it, knowing that with or without the slugs the twelve men he'd injected would be dead in six hours.

The saline solution would cause the fluid to move more quickly through their veins, spreading the infection at maximum speed.

The small red areas around the needle marks began to itch less than fifteen minutes after the men had left the lab, and more than one of them felt a dull pain growing at the base of his skull.

The infection was already beginning to set in.

At 12.03 p.m., the first of the twelve men climbed down the metal ladder towards the black maw of the tunnel beneath Shaftesbury Avenue.

Thirty-four

Alan Finch wiped the perspiration from his face and sighed. The sun seemed even hotter today. It beat down on the city like a red-hot hammer.

Next to him, Lisa stood with her head lowered slightly, straining her ears to hear the sometimes muffled voices filtering through the army radio set up in the rear of a truck. It was parked next to one of the massive Scanias which supported a KVA 1000. The generator was still humming its tuneless refrain.

DI Grogan pushed another cigarette into his mouth and fumbled in his pocket for a match. He didn't have one.

Maconnell pulled out a lighter and lit the policeman's Marlboro for him.

A voice came from the radio again, fighting against the static.

'... no sign ... any kind of movement down here,' the voice said. '... our bloke or the slugs ... so dark ... difficult to see very far ahead even with ... torches.'

Maconnell motioned for the radio operator to hand him the microphone.

'Unit One, come in.'

The set crackled again, like someone walking on cornflakes.

'Unit One. I read ... but ... hard to hear ... signal keeps breaking up.'

'How far are you from us?' the Captain wanted to know.

'... Difficult ... reckon about three hund ... yards ... a little less.' The signal broke up completely.

'Unit One, repeat,' said Maconnell, becoming agitated.

More wild hissing. Static.

'Do you read me?'

'I hear you, sir ... just about ... we ... to a bend in the tunnel ... away to the right ...'

'Can't you do anything about this?' the officer snapped, looking angrily at the radio operator.

The man fiddled with the controls but his efforts paid little dividend.

'What if the slugs don't follow them?' said Lisa.

'They will,' Finch assured her, his voice low.

Grogan took another hefty drag on his cigarette, blowing out a long stream of smoke a moment later. He tugged on his tie, loosening it slightly.

'Unit One, to Command.'

The voice came over with momentary but startling clarity, making those nearby jump.

Maconnell snatched the microphone from the radio operator.

'This is Command. Come in,' he said.

'Sir ... there's something ... tunnel behind us. I can't see what it is ... one of the other blokes is going to check it out ... splashing about ... it could be ...'

Finch, Lisa and Grogan all turned to listen as the voice on the other end of the line rose in pitch, the sound now clearly audible between short bursts of static.

'. . . Jesus Christ . . . there's thousands of them . . . they're in the water . . . on the walls . . . MOVE NOW . . .' A scream. 'Slugs everywhere . . . if we can make it to the next sewer exit . . . where the fuck is it? . . .' Another scream, louder. 'Oh Jesus, Jesus . . . I've dropped my torch . . . the slugs are everywhere . . . where's the . . .'

Another voice, in pain, in agony.

'HELP ME . . .'

'. . . Captain . . . where's the exit . . . they're all over us . . . oh JESUS . . . JESUS . . .' Another scream, one which made the hairs on the back of Finch's neck stand up.

'. . . WE CAN'T GET OUT . . . NO . . . OH GOD THEY'RE ON MY FACE . . . MY EYES . . . MY EYES . . .'

The shrieks which issued forth could have come from hell itself.

'. . . MY EYES . . . MY EYES . . .'

'Turn it off,' Maconnell rasped at the wireless operator.

The man hesitated a second and the officer bellowed the order again.

The sound of the screams was cut off.

An unearthly silence descended but the echo of the shrieks seemed to hang in the air like accusations.

'Oh God,' Lisa said, softly.

Finch and Maconnell exchanged glances which seemed tinged with a mixture of guilt and sorrow.

'What about the other men?' the doctor wanted to know. 'Can you contact them?'

For long moments the officer seemed lost in thought, the screams of agony still ringing all too loudly in his ears, then he nodded, shaking himself from the great weariness which had settled over him. He told the radio operator to contact the second group of men, the unit moving along the storm-relief sewer from Brewer Street. The operator began fiddling with the controls of the machine.

Private Terry Banks held his rifle across his chest as he paddled his way through the knee-high water. The man beside him, whom he knew only as Jenkins, was holding a powerful torch in one hand and a two-way radio in the other. Behind them, Chas Granger and a tall, red-haired Scot called Lewis followed, both of them occasionally peering back over their shoulders into the almost palpable blackness. Lewis pulled the torch from his belt and flicked it on, playing the beam over the walls of the tunnel behind them. It illuminated only dark, festering green mould.

'Anything up ahead?' Lewis asked as the men waded on.

'Not yet,' Jenkins said, a note of anxiety in his voice.

'How the fuck do we know we're going in the right direction?' Lewis asked.

'Keep heading straight, they told us,' said Banks, trying to breathe through his nose to minimise the rancid stench of the effluent. 'That's right, isn't it, Chas?'

His voice echoed around the tunnel.

Granger didn't answer.

'Chas.'

'What?' he snapped, his voice low and gravelly.

'They told us to keep going straight ahead,' Banks repeated, glancing back at his companion.

Granger nodded, but as he did so, he felt the pain which had fastened itself around the base of his skull like an iron fist gripping a little tighter and he winced. His skin felt as if someone had rubbed hot ash all over it, and there was perspiration on his forehead.

On one cheek two large boils were beginning to form.

'How far to Piccadilly?' Lewis wanted to know. 'These tunnels give me the shits.'

Banks laughed, a hollow chuckle which gradually died away into the silence.

'Well, if you get the shits, there's no better place to be than down a sewer,' he said.

'Yeah, highly amusing,' Lewis said. 'How far to go?'

'I reckon about eight or nine hundred yards,' Banks told him.

They moved on, Jenkins almost slipping over in the murky river of effluent. The radio in his hand suddenly erupted into life and he raised it to his ear.

'Unit Two, come in.'

They recognized the voice as Maconnell's.

'Unit Two. We hear you, sir,' Jenkins answered. 'There's still no sign of the slugs.'

There was an uncomfortable pause, then Maconnell spoke again.

'We've lost Unit One,' he said simply.

'Oh Jesus,' Terry Banks murmured.

'Maintain your progress towards Piccadilly,' the Captain told them. 'The generators are set up.'

'Generators?' said Lewis. 'What the fuck are they going to do with generators?'

Jenkins waved a hand for the big Scot to be silent.

'Understood, sir,' he said into the two-way.

'Leave this frequency open,' Maconnell said.

Then there was silence again, broken only by the splashing of the men as they battled through the reeking water.

Granger slowed his pace, the pain at the base of his skull now spreading quickly, reaching up over the back of his head and temples until it was hammering like an out-of-control pneumatic drill. He clenched his teeth.

Another large blister had formed on his neck and, beneath his uniform he could feel others chafing against the material. He put out a hand to steady himself, touching the slimy walls. Some of the slick mould stuck to his palm but it did not seem to bother him.

He glanced across at Lewis, then forward to the men ahead of him. To Jenkins with the radio and the torch and to Banks, who still held his automatic rifle across his chest.

Granger's right hand dropped to his belt, his fingers closing around the haft of his bayonet. He began to ease it from its sheath.

'Look,' Jenkins said, shining the torch back and forth.

'Which one do we take?' Lewis asked.

The tunnel curved around to the right but there was another slightly smaller outlet to the left. Filthy water was running fairly rapidly from this other tunnel, joining the main flow. The men moved on until they were level with the second tunnel and Jenkins shone the torch inside. The beam was swallowed up by the darkness after about ten yards. What lay beyond that impenetrable wall of gloom no one knew.

'I say we stay in this tunnel,' said Banks, trying to swallow but not managing it. His mouth and throat were parched. There was a dull, insistent ache at the back of his neck which seemed to be intensifying.

'I agree,' Lewis said hurriedly, anxious to move away from the gaping black mouth and its untold secrets. Secrets which none of them cared to know.

'If we take a wrong turning we're fucked,' Banks said worriedly. 'The slugs will cut us off.'

Granger eased the bayonet free of its sheath, his eyes bulging wildly in their sockets as he studied his three companions. One of the blisters on his cheek had ruptured and he could feel thick liquid running down his skin.

'Perhaps I should check with the Captain,' Jenkins offered.

'Fuck the Captain,' snapped Banks. 'He's not down here. I say we push on.'

Something thick and heavy bumped against the private's leg and he shouted in sudden, unexpected fear, his voice reverberating around the tunnel.

The other men tensed, fearing the worst.

All except Granger who was clutching the bayonet in a talon-like grip.

Banks looked down, moving back slightly, his heart thudding madly against his ribs.

'What is it?' Jenkins said, his voice a hoarse whisper.

'It's a bloody turd, that's what it is,' Banks said, breathing a sigh of relief. He turned to look at Granger. 'What about that . . .'

He got no further.

The bayonet flashed forward, driven with demonic strength by Granger.

As Banks opened his mouth to protest, the blade was thrust past his lips, powering into the roof of his mouth, shattering several teeth on its passage. The vicious blade tore up through his pallet, lacerating his gums and nearly severing his bottom lip as it was torn free.

The second thrust punctured his throat just below the right ear, releasing a thick fountain of blood. Granger felt the bayonet grate on bone as he twisted it, heedless of the hot fluid which splashed him.

He turned next on Lewis, who tried to swing his rifle around in an effort to cover himself. But Granger moved with surprising agility in the knee-deep effluent. He pulled the Scot towards him, driving the bayonet into his stomach just below the navel, dragging the blade upwards until it cracked against Lewis' sternum. His stomach opened like a grinning mouth, the ragged edges of the wound stretching wide as his intestines spilled forward in a steaming tangle which made a loud splash in the filthy water. Bile, thick and green, came spilling from his slashed bladder and the Scot jerked in uncontrollable spasms as he attempted to push his innards back into the hideous rent.

With a strangled cry he fell forward, his body disappearing beneath the surface.

Jenkins took his chance and ran but the water held him back and more than once he slipped and almost fell. With the weight of water against him it was as if he were running in slow motion, every step half its normal speed. He did not look back. He did not *dare* look back but he could hear the water splashing and churning as Granger pursued him, the bayonet still in his hand.

Jenkins began to moan in terror as he heard his pursuer gaining, and in his mind's eye he could see the blade descending towards his unprotected back. He still held the torch, its light bouncing around madly as he ran.

He knew he had only one chance.

Jenkins turned and swung the heavy flashlight.

It struck Granger on the temple, causing one of the boils there to burst violently. An explosion of pus spewed from the punctured boil. The impact seemed only to stun Granger momentarily, and he kept coming.

Jenkins lashed out again. This time, his attacker ducked beneath the swing, driving the blade upwards. The point punctured Jenkins' flesh in the hollow of his armpit, tearing away some muscle as it twisted free. His arm went numb and he dropped the radio into the water. He could feel blood pouring from the wound and he backed off, holding the torch before him defiantly, its beam now illuminating Granger's bloodied, blistered face. His eyes blazed maniacally as he advanced once more.

This time Jenkins brought the torch down on Granger's shoulder but the crazed man's momentum carried him forward and both of them toppled over, the stinking brown water closing over them. A flood of filth filled Jenkins' nose and mouth and his stomach contracted violently, but before he could even try to raise himself he felt something sharp being pressed against his neck.

The bayonet sliced through muscle and veins, hacking through his carotid artery with ease.

Granger rose from beneath the water like some creature from a horror film, a swamp-bred monstrosity dripping blood and stinking water. He stood motionless for a moment, then turned and headed back towards the branch tunnel, moving quickly through the water into its enveloping blackness.

This tunnel was much narrower, and when he extended both arms he was able to touch the two sides without much difficulty. He ploughed on, blind in the darkness, moving as if by instinct. But if that instinct was correct, he should soon find what he sought.

Another two or three minutes and he was there.

The metal ladder stretched upwards towards the surface.

Towards light. Away from this stinking sewer.

Away from the slugs.

Granger was in severe pain. The steady gnawing at the base of his skull had become a raging ache. The blisters which covered his face and body throbbed and pulsed, many of them leaking pus. Nevertheless, the bayonet tucked in his belt, he began to climb. When he reached the top of the ladder he paused, sucking in deep, rasping breaths. When he coughed he tasted the foul sewer water and he hawked loudly, bringing it up, retching violently in an effort to rid himself of the effluent which he'd swallowed. He hung from the ladder a moment longer, teeth gritted against the pain. Slowly, he raised the manhole cover an inch or two.

Bright sunlight flooded into his eyes and he nearly dropped the steel lid. Peering around him after his eyes began to adjust to the brilliance, he saw that the street into which he'd emerged was deserted.

Except for the solitary army truck which was parked by the kerb.

Its driver was leaning against the cab door smoking a roll-up.

He had his back to Granger.

The private slid back the manhole cover further, cursing when it grated against the road surface, but the driver did not hear the sound. He continued puffing away at his cigarette.

Granger slid from the hole and rolled once, darting for cover in a nearby shop doorway. He looked up and spotted a street sign. There was a white arrow and one word on it:

PICCADILLY

Granger smiled crookedly, tasting something bitter which rolled from a large blister on his top lip.

He hefted the bayonet before him for a moment, then pulled the automatic rifle from his shoulder, clipping the blade to the end of the barrel. He checked the firing mechanism on the FN, ensuring that its brief spell beneath the water hadn't hampered it in any way. He ejected a shell, pleased to see that the action was as smooth as he'd hoped. He slipped the safety catch to 'OFF'.

The driver of the army truck continued smoking, oblivious to the movement behind him.

Granger guessed that there were some fifteen yards between himself and the unsuspecting driver.

Lowering the rifle, he moved forward, his eyes never leaving the driver's unprotected back.

A twisted smile spread across his ravaged face.

Thirty-five

'We've lost Number Two Unit as well, sir,' the radio operator told Maconnell, his face colouring as if he were personally to blame.

The captain slammed his fist down hard on the running board of the truck and sucked in a despairing breath.

'What now?' he said, angrily.

'Throw the switches,' Finch urged him. 'Activate the generators. If the slugs are down there it doesn't matter exactly how close they are, the electricity should kill them, anyway.'

'There are still men down there, sir,' the radio operator said.

Maconnell ignored him and turned to look at Finch.

'Give the order,' the doctor said. 'Now.'

'There's enough power here to wipe out millions of the fucking things,' Grogan added, almost excitedly.

For all he knew there *were* millions.

'Give the order,' Finch urged again, moving closer to the captain.

'But the men down there . . .' the radio operator protested once more.

'They're better off dead,' Maconnell whispered.

'*Then do it*,' Finch almost shouted, feeling as if he should shake the officer.

'Standby to activate the generators,' the captain roared, his powerful voice heard by everyone gathered around the now deathly-silent hub of London, Piccadilly Circus. The civilian engineers in charge of the generators waited for the final order, their machines humming like millions of angry bees. The air itself seemed to crackle with the energy waiting to be unleashed. Lisa moved closer to Finch, sensing that the time had come.

The six KVA 1000's rumbled ominously and Finch half expected to see a glow surrounding the big trucks which held them. He tried to swallow but he found that his mouth was too dry.

Grogan dropped his cigarette end and stamped on it, glancing first at Maconnell, then at the network of cables which snaked across the Circus to be swallowed up by the manhole.

Captain Maconnell exhaled almost painfully, praying that this last desperate gambit would work. He raised one arm as a signal.

'Ready,' he roared.

At that instant they all heard the screams.

For a moment no one was sure where they were coming from. Then all eyes turned towards the manhole.

The screams of agony grew louder, and for brief seconds that seemed interminable, everything and everyone froze.

Corporal Simon Johnson dragged himself from the hole and staggered a few yards, arms outstretched like a sleep-walker.

Slugs, dozens of them, clung to Johnson's face and body, eating into him as he walked.

Somehow he stayed upright on legs which had been almost eaten away by the ravenous black creatures. Blood splattered the concrete around him as he stumbled onward, trying to tug the monstrosities from his ravaged body. He had hold of one which had eaten through his left eye and, as the horrified men watched, he pulled it from the riven cavity, tugging the swollen, slimy form inch by inch from the socket as if he were drawing some huge splinter from his skin. The slug was coated with blood and vitreous liquid and it filled the empty orifice almost completely. Still screaming, despite the fact that two of the slugs were inside his mouth feasting on his tongue, Johnson tottered towards the nearest group of men, his shaking hand finally pulling the other beast free from the hole in his skull. As he dropped it, he stepped on the fat shape and it burst in a shower of dark fluid.

Maconnell stepped forward, pulled the Browning from its holster and aimed. He fired once, the heavy-grain bullet taking the top of Johnson's head off. He went down in a heap, the slugs still slithering over him, some seething into the open cavity of his skull, anxious to reach the greyish-red brain now exposed by the ferocity of the bullet's exit.

Maconnell fired again, then turned away in disgust.

'Throw the switches,' he bellowed.

Finch held tightly to Lisa as the generators were activated and the first surge of power hurtled along the cables and into the sewers. There was a loud crackling which grew in pitch until it seemed to fill the air. The doctor felt his hair stand on end as electricity hissed and spluttered around him. The trucks which held the generators seemed to vibrate as the incredible power was unleashed. Over 30,000 volts was produced and more than one of the machines became hot as the power level was sustained.

In the sewers the cables danced madly in the water like the limbs of some huge over-active octopus. Slugs close by were destroyed instantly, their bodies swelling and exploding. The current whipped through the tunnels, seeking each one of them out. Their thick bodies stiffened, then collapsed, spilling reeking fluids and slime into the already rancid water.

The air inside the tunnels glowed with a dull blue light and the water itself bubbled like a geyser as it heated up. Several pockets of methane gas, ignited by the sparks, burst into flames and those watching saw tongues of fire licking briefly from the manhole. It was followed by a great brownish-white cloud of steam which covered the whole of Piccadilly Circus in an impenetrable fog. The smell of ozone was so powerful it made Finch and some of the others cough.

And still the generators roared, the cables whiplashing as the power continued to surge through them.

For a full ten minutes the electrical barrage was sustained. Then, moving from truck to truck, Maconnell gave the order for them to be shut down. Gradually, silence descended again, except for the occasional sound of coughing.

The noxious cloud of steam gradually dissipated and, once again, those in the concrete arena found themselves at the mercy of the sun.

Two soldiers near the corpse of Johnson moved forward, crushing the slugs on or near his body with their heavy boots.

'Now we wait,' the captain said, his voice low. 'Another thirty minutes and *I'll* take some men down to check the tunnels.'

'What if it hasn't worked?' asked Grogan, lighting another cigarette.

His question hung unanswered in the air, like the last vestiges of the steam.

'I just hope the other men were dead before the slugs reached them,' Maconnell said wearily. He slid the Browning back into its holster and leant on the bonnet of his Landrover.

Finch looked at his watch.

It was exactly one o'clock. In the distance, they heard the familiar chime of Big Ben, normally inaudible for anyone in Piccadilly Circus at that time of the day, but in the unusual silence the sound carried. The single strike was sounded, then died on the warm breeze which had sprung up. A wind of change, thought Finch, wondering why the thought seemed so amusing. He held Lisa close to him.

The oppressive silence was suddenly broken by the roar of a lorry engine.

Thirty-six

Taking the truck had been so easy, thought Chas Granger as

211

he stomped down on the accelerator.

The driver hadn't even heard him as he'd approached stealthily from behind. Only when the rifle had been pressed to the back of his head had he reacted, and by then, of course, it was too late. The close-range blast had ripped away most of the back and top of his skull, spraying blood, bone and fragments of brain up the side of the truck's cab. Granger had taken the keys from the dead man and started the huge vehicle up. Now, hunched over the wheel, he was travelling down Regent Street with the needle on the speedo touching seventy.

Around the next corner, he thought. Yes, sure enough, there was the first of the big Scania lorries. He could see troops scurrying around it, some even taking up firing positions, but he merely aimed the army truck at the rear of the first lorry and ducked down.

The impact when it came, was horrendous but the truck ploughed on, ripping most of the back half of the Scania away in an explosion of twisted metal. Men unwary enough to be caught in his path were flattened by the juggernaught, which roared on into the heart of Piccadilly Circus, bowling men over like skittles, crushing some of them beneath its huge wheels. Granger heard their screams and felt the almost imperceptible bumps as they were crushed to pulp beneath the truck, but with no more concern than if they had been insects.

Two shots smacked into the side window, shattering it. Glass sprayed into the cab and one of the bullets nicked his ear, tearing off the lobe. Still he drove on, aiming the lorry at a clutch of smaller vehicles parked in front of him.

Finch had seen the truck smash through the troops and lorries and now he pulled Lisa aside as it bore down on them.

Maconnell drew his Browning again, squeezing off three rounds, the second of which shattered the truck's windscreen. The glass spiderwebbed but Granger knocked a hole in it with one dripping fist, his foot still pressed firmly down on the accelerator.

He crashed into Finch's Chevette, crumpling up the car as if it had been made of paper. The doctor pulled Lisa down as a portion of the front bumper spun through the air like lethal shrapnel.

'The petrol tank,' Grogan yelled, seeing golden fluid spilling from the wreck. The DI ran for cover, seeing Finch and Lisa ahead of him.

It was a stray bullet which ignited the fuel.

There was an ear-splitting roar, followed immediately by a high-pitched scream as the petrol went up. A mushroom cloud of yellow and red flames erupted from the twisted hulk, billowing out thick black smoke. Blazing petrol spread across Piccadilly Circus like a huge fiery amoeba, reaching out to engulf anyone nearby.

The heat wave sent Lisa hurtling through the air despite Finch's efforts to hold onto her. She was blown like a leaf in an autumn wind, crashing into the side of Maconnell's Landrover with a sickening thump. A gash fully five inches wide opened across her forehead and blood spilled down her face. The doctor was catapulted into the air too, but he was more fortunate. He hit the concrete and rolled, coming to a stop with little more than a cut beneath his left eye. He immediately scrambled to his feet and rushed across to Lisa, pulling a handkerchief from his pocket. He folded it up and pressed it to the wound, cradling her head with his other hand.

DI Grogan ran to his own car and leapt behind the wheel, twisting the key hard in the ignition. He jammed the car into gear and stepped on the accelerator. The wheels spun wildly on the concrete for a second, then the Volvo shot forward as if fired from a cannon. In his rear-view mirror he caught sight of Maconnell following in the Landrover. The two vehicles sped after the fleeing truck, which was now roaring up Shaftesbury Avenue.

Just before they reached Cambridge Circus, Grogan managed to draw alongside the large truck. He could see the driver almost slumped over the wheel, his face a patchwork of boils and welts

Granger twisted the wheel of the truck and slammed it into the Volvo.

The car mounted the pavement and sideswiped a building but Grogan remained in control of the vehicle. He heard metal scrape against concrete and saw sparks flying from the side of the car as he struggled to get it back on the road. He thanked God that this part of the city had been evacuated.

As he swerved back onto the road, Maconnell drove past in the Landrover. He too drew alongside the truck, but as it turned to ram him he wrenched his own wheel and guided his vehicle out of danger. There was a scream of tyres as the two of them skidded violently but the Captain recovered first and fired two shots from his Browning.

The first hit the windowframe of the truck's cab, the second ricocheted off the wing with a loud squeal.

Cursing, Granger stuck the barrel of his rifle out of the shattered window and fired a short burst. Bullets spattered the Landrover, one of them blasting off the door handle, another blowing in part of the windscreen. A third caught Maconnell in the shoulder.

He grunted at the thudding impact, almost losing control of the Landrover as white-hot pain enveloped his arm. He felt blood running down the throbbing limb but he managed to hold onto the steering wheel, and as the lorry, the Landrover and the Volvo all roared up Charing Cross Road, they were racing level.

Grogan looked anxiously at the truck, moving away from it every so often in case the crazed driver should decide to ram him, but Granger seemed to ignore the pursuing vehicles for a moment. A wave of pain so intense he almost blacked out had swept through him, and he moaned as he felt the large pustule above his right eye burst, the sticky fluid almost blinding him. He wiped it away with the back of his hand, pressing down ever harder on the truck's accelerator as if trying to push it through the floor of the cab.

Gritting his teeth against his own pain, Maconnell aimed his automatic once more and, this time, he kept firing.

The first shot sped across the bonnet of the truck. The

214

second hit Granger in the side. He screamed in pain and the truck swerved, pushing the Volvo towards an oncoming bus shelter.

Grogan ducked low as his car hit the obstacle.

There was a deafening explosion of glass as the structure disintegrated, huge shards of crystal flying in all directions, some smashing through the windscreen of the policeman's car. A particularly long piece speared his left forearm, scraping the bone as it passed through, laying muscles open.

Somehow, the DI kept control of the car, aware now that they were nearing the intersection with Oxford Street.

From inside the Landrover, Maconnell squeezed off more shots.

One hit the dashboard of the truck, the next blew away part of the wing mirror.

It was the third shot the captain fired which proved to be lethal.

Moving at a speed in excess of 900 feet per second, the bullet slammed into Granger's face, ripping away most of his bottom jaw before blasting a fist-sized exit hole in the other side of his head. Blood and brain tissue exploded from the wound and coated the inside of the cab. The corpse slumped forward and, too late, Maconnell realized what was going to happen.

The big truck veered to one side, skewing into the Landrover. The bumpers of the two vehicles locked, sealing them together as surely as if they'd been welded.

The officer wrestled with the steering wheel in an effort to extricate the Landrover, but it was useless.

The wide glass doors of the Dominion Theatre loomed ahead.

Behind, Grogan stepped hard on his brakes, the Volvo spinning round in the middle of the road. He looked up in time to see the truck and its reluctant companion smash into the theatre.

They burst through the doors, ploughing on into the foyer, where seconds later they exploded. A roaring tide of fire erupted from within and Grogan ducked as his car was bombarded with lumps of debris. Pieces of glass rained down, shattering on the concrete with a series of loud crashes. The theatre's canopy, which boasted of forthcoming events, collapsed amidst a cloud of smoke and dust and there were fresh explosions as the lights inside went up. Thick, choking fumes belched from the theatre, momentarily blotting out the sun as they formed a massive dark cloud. As Grogan clambered out of his car, gripping his slashed forearm, he could feel the heat from the flames which danced and leapt around the devastated vehicles.

He heard the sound of car engines from behind him and looked round to see another Landrover and two army lorries speeding towards the scene of destruction. He noticed that there was a blue Cortina with them, and as it pulled up he saw Finch and DS Nicholson get out. Both of them looked across at the burning theatre.

'Get on the blower,' Grogan shouted to the DS. 'Get a fire engine here, quick, before the whole fucking street goes up in flames.'

'And an ambulance,' Finch called, seeing the severity of the wound on Grogan's arm.

'Is Miss Foster all right?' the policeman wanted to know.

Finch nodded.

'They've taken her to hospital. It's a bad cut but she'll be fine once they get some stitches in it.' He looked across at the flames which were still leaping from the front of the theatre. 'What about Maconnell?'

'He burned up in that lot, poor bastard.'

Finch sighed. 'Those sewer tunnels will have to be checked,' he said quietly.

Grogan nodded. He leant back against the bonnet of his car, the pain in his arm now raging.

'There could be others infected with the disease,' he said.

'The area was searched. They would have been found.'

'I hope you're right,' the DI said wearily.

Finch looked back at the burning building, at the troops who milled around it, at the glass and other debris strewn across the road.

216

'The newspapers will have a field day,' he said. 'What's happened in the past week should keep them going for months. Man-eating slugs.' He laughed humourlessly. 'I can't wait to see the headlines.'

He stopped staring at the fire for a moment longer and then closed his eyes, wishing he could blot out not only the sight before him but also the horrors that had gone before.

Finch knew that was not to be. What he'd seen in the last few days was burned indelibly into his memory, never to be erased.

When he opened his eyes again, Grogan had passed out.

'Where's that bloody ambulance?' the doctor yelled at Nicholson, dropping to one knee to tend to the injured DI as best he could.

High above them, like a circlet of burnished gold, the sun continued to shine.

Epilogue

Theresa Finch walked back towards the Renault, juggling an armful of soft-drink cans and food cartons, muttering to herself as hot grease from one of the hamburgers dripped onto her fingers.

A dog, shut inside a yellow Mini, barked at her as she passed. It pressed its face to one of the windows as if trying to escape the stifling confines of the car.

The car park outside the Little Chef was full of vehicles. Everything from motorbikes to eighteen-wheelers, all baking in the brilliant sunshine.

She had left London Sunday morning, after unsuccessfully trying to persuade Richard to join her and Christopher. She had driven north, towards her parents' home in Cumbria near the Scottish border, breaking the long journey with an overnight stop. It was now mid-day Monday and they would be there in an hour or two.

Perhaps her ex-husband had been right about the mysterious disease. Theresa didn't know for sure but she'd decided not to take any chances. Despite what she might think of him, Alan, she knew loved Chris more than anything else in the world.

Chris hadn't complained about the sudden departure. In fact, he'd seemed quite excited about the whole venture. As they'd continued the journey today, though, he'd become quieter and more subdued.

Now, as his mother reached the Renault, she saw him gazing listlessly out of the open side window.

'Here you are, love,' she said, handing him his Coke and

hamburger. Theresa slid into the driver's seat, fidgeting as she felt the hot plastic against her skin. She took a swig from her own can of Diet Pepsi and smiled at her son.

'Have we got far to go, Mum?' he asked her.

'Not far,' she told him, brushing some strands of blond, almost silver, hair from his forehead.

He looked up at her and smiled, a bit wanly.

Theresa noticed how red his face and arms were. The sun must be even stronger than she'd thought.

Chris ate half the hamburger and washed it down with gulps of Coke. When he finished he sat back in his seat, wishing that the pain at the base of his skull would go away.

On his right shoulder, hidden beneath his T-shirt, the first two blisters were beginning to form.

NEMESIS

Shaun Hutson

Sue and John Hackett are contemplating the ruins of their marriage. The brutal murder of their young daughter has brought an already strained relationship to breaking point, and to try to salvage their lives they retreat to the small peaceful town of Hinkston. But Hinkston isn't peaceful any more. It's being torn apart by a series of horrific, unexplained murders. And it holds a fateful, fifty-year-old secret – a secret with such appalling consequences that it was supposed to have died during the war. It didn't . . .

HORROR
0 7474 0789 4

EREBUS

Shaun Hutson

Wakely was just a small farming community but something was terribly wrong there. Something wrong with the livestock, with the people. Something unspeakable. Perpetuated by the mysterious Venderburg Chemicals Group who sought to protect its interests and secrets no matter what the cost to the people of Wakely, or indeed, to the rest of mankind. And who would have thought that red meat could be so deadly . . . ?

HORROR
0 7474 0783 5

SHADOWS

Shaun Hutson

Enter the domain of chaos, insanity and death . . . In Oxford and Paris psychic investigators are attempting to probe forbidden areas of the mind. In New York writer David Blake is studying the methods of miracle healer Jonathon Mathias. Driven by their own desperate motives, these researchers are about to unlock Pandora's Box. To unleash the horrifying forces of destruction hidden deep within us all . . .

HORROR
0 7474 0785 1

All Sphere Books are available at your bookshop or newsagent, or can be ordered from the following address: Sphere Books, Cash Sales Department, P.O. Box 11, Falmouth, Cornwall TR10 9EN.

Please send cheque or postal order (no currency), and allow 60p for postage and packing for the first book plus 25p for the second book and 15p for each additional book ordered up to a maximum charge of £1.90 in U.K.

B.F.P.O. customers allow 60p for the first book, 25p for the second book plus 15p per copy for the next 7 books thereafter 9p per book.

Overseas customers, including Eire, please allow £1.25 for postage and packing for the first book, 75p for the second book and 28p for each subsequent title ordered.